Just Plain Foolishness

RACHEL YODER—
Always Trouble Somewhere

Book 6

WANDA E.
BRUNSTETTER

BARBOUR
PUBLISHING

Cover artist: Richard Hoit

For more information about Wanda E. Brunstetter, please access the author's Web site at the following Internet address: www.wandabrunstetter.com

Published by Barbour Publishing, Inc., P.O. Box 719, Uhrichsville, Ohio 44683, www.barbourbooks.com

Our mission is to publish and distribute inspirational products offering exceptional value and biblical encouragement to the masses.

 Member of the
Evangelical Christian
Publishers Association

Printed in the United States of America.

Dedication

To Ella Schrock. Thanks for letting me tour
your wonderful greenhouse.
To the children and teachers at the Pine Creek Amish
schoolhouse in Goshen, Indiana. I enjoyed meeting you
and introducing you to my Grandma Yoder puppet.
And to Elvera Kienbaum. Thanks for sharing
your wonderful strawberry story with me.

Other books by Wanda E. Brunstetter

Fiction

Rachel Yoder—Always Trouble Somewhere Series
School's Out!
Back to School
Out of Control
A Happy Heart
Just Plain Foolishness

Sisters of Holmes County Series

Brides of Webster County Series

Daughters of Lancaster County Series

Brides of Lancaster County Series

Nonfiction
Wanda Brunstetter's Amish Friends Cookbook
The Simple Life

Glossary

ach—oh
aebeer—strawberry
aebier—strawberries
alt—old
bensel—silly child
boppli—baby
bopplin—babies
brieder—brothers
bruder—brother
busslin—kittens
buwe—boy
daed—dad
danki—thanks
dechder—daughters
dumm—dumb
gans—goose
grossdaadi—grandfather
gut—good
hund—dog
jah—yes
kapp—cap
kinner—children
kumme—come
maedel—girl
mamm—mom
maus—mouse
meis—mice
naerfich—nervous
schee—pretty
schissel—bowl
schliffer—splinter

schmaert—smart
schnell—quickly
schtinkich—stuffy
schwach—feeble
schweschder—sister
sei so gut—please
shillgrott—turtle
windel—diaper
wunderbaar—wonderful

Bisht du an schlaufa?	Are you sleeping?
Schweschder Hannah	Sister Hannah
Ich hei-ah die bells an ringa.	Morning bells are ringing.
Des kann ich finne.	I can find it.
Die Rachel is die ganz zeit am grumble.	Rachel is grumbling all the time.
Dummel dich net!	Take your time! Don't hurry!
Geb's mir!	Give it to me!
Guder mariye.	Good morning.
Gut nacht.	Good night.
Grummel net um mich rum.	Don't grumble around me.
Hallich gebottsdaag.	Happy birthday.
Hoscht du schunn geese?	Have you already eaten?
Letscht nacht hab ich ohreweh ghat.	I had an earache last night.
She dich, eich, wider!	See you later!
Was in der welt?	What in all the world?
Wie geht's?	How are you?

Contents

Chapter 1
Grandpa's Greenhouse

Bang! Bang! Bang!

Rachel Yoder stepped onto the back porch and shielded her eyes from the glare of the morning sun. She was excited to see Grandpa Schrock's new greenhouse going up on the front of Pap's property. More than a dozen men from their Amish community had come to help.

Pap, Henry, and other men kept busy pounding nails into the wood framing, while Rudy and another group of men sawed the lumber. Rachel's brother Jacob and several other boys carried lumber and other supplies to the men. Grandpa helped wherever he could and supervised everything.

"I wish I could help build Grandpa's greenhouse," Rachel said when Mom stepped onto the porch with a jug of water and a stack of paper cups. "It looks like the men are having so much fun."

Mom nodded, and her glasses slipped to the end of her nose. Rachel was glad her own blue plastic-framed glasses stayed in place. But that was probably because the bridge of her nose wasn't as thin as Mom's nose.

"I'm sure the men enjoy what they're doing, but it's a lot of hard work," Mom said, pushing her glasses back in place. "That's why we need to keep taking snacks and cold drinks to them."

She handed Rachel the jug of water and paper cups. "Would you please take these out to the workers? They must be thirsty by now."

Rachel groaned. "Do I have to carry water? I'd rather help build the greenhouse."

"That's just plain foolishness, Rachel. Hammering nails and sawing wood is men's work." Mom nudged Rachel's arm. "Now hurry and take this water to the workers."

Gripping the handle of the water jug in one hand, and holding the package of paper cups under her arm, Rachel stepped off the porch.

Her bare feet tingled as she trudged through the cool grass. When she reached the graveled driveway, she walked carefully so she wouldn't step on any sharp rocks. Halfway there, she met Jacob.

"How are things going with Grandpa's greenhouse?" she asked.

"Real well. I'll bet we'll have it up before the day's out." He motioned to the entrance of the building being framed with wood. The rest of the greenhouse would be built with plastic pipe and covered with heavy plastic.

Rachel sighed. "I wish I could help build the greenhouse. It's not fair that you get to have all the fun."

Jacob grunted and wiped a trickle of sweat running down his forehead. "*Jah* [Yes], right. Helping build the greenhouse is not all fun and games, sister. It's hard work—men's work!"

She snickered. "What would you know about men's work? You're not a man."

Jacob puffed out his chest and lifted his chin. "I'll be thirteen years old in a few months. Before long I'll graduate from school and start helping Pap on the farm full-time—just two more years."

"I'll turn eleven before you turn thirteen," Rachel said. "In case you've forgotten, my birthday's only a few weeks away."

Jacob shrugged. "You're still two years younger than me. That means I'm a lot smarter than you are."

"No, it doesn't."

"Jah, it does."

Rachel shook her head. "Grandpa thinks I'm *schmaert* [smart]. If he didn't, he wouldn't have said I could help him in the greenhouse after it's built."

Jacob snorted. "That doesn't mean you're schmaert. It just means you'll be busy in the greenhouse. Maybe that will help you stay out of trouble for a change."

"What's that supposed to mean?"

"Trouble seems to follow wherever you go. Always trouble somewhere. Isn't that what you say?"

Rachel shrugged. "I guess that's true, but I'm hoping I'll have less trouble and more fun after Grandpa's greenhouse is open for business."

"We'll see about that." Jacob motioned to the lumber pile on the other side of the driveway. "I'd better get more wood for the men who are building."

"Can I carry some wood?" Rachel asked.

Jacob shook his head. "If you want to help, stick with what you're doing and see that everyone gets plenty of water."

Rachel frowned. "What's so helpful about hauling water?"

"It helps the thirsty men," Jacob called as he sprinted up the driveway.

When Rachel arrived at the worksite, she set

the water and paper cups on the piece of plywood being used as a table.

"I brought you some water," Rachel said when she spotted Grandpa near the entrance of his greenhouse.

He smiled. "*Danki* [Thanks]. I could use a cool drink about now."

"How's everything going?" she asked after he'd helped himself to a cup of water.

"Real well. I think we should have my greenhouse finished by the end of the day."

"Sure wish I could help build it," Rachel said. "It would be a lot more fun than hauling water or helping Mom make sandwiches and lemonade."

Grandpa raised his bushy gray eyebrows high. "Sorry, Rachel, but building the greenhouse is hard work—too hard for a young girl like you." He patted Rachel's back. "You'll get to help me inside the greenhouse once it's open for business."

"How soon will that be?" she asked.

"Probably in a week or two. I need time to get everything set up."

"Will it be open before Mom has her *boppli* [baby]?"

"Probably so," he said with a nod. "Unless the baby decides to appear early."

Rachel thrust out her bottom lip. "I hope it doesn't come early."

Grandpa tipped his head. "You're not anxious to see your little *bruder* [brother] or *schweschder* [sister]?"

"I—I guess so, but I'm more anxious to help in your greenhouse. If Mom doesn't keep me too busy with chores, that is." Rachel frowned. "I'm afraid once the boppli comes I'll have more chores to do than ever."

Grandpa tweaked Rachel's nose. "I'm sure you'll have some free time to help me."

Pap stepped up to the table and greeted Rachel with a smile. "I see you brought us some water." He poured some into a paper cup and drank. "Ah. . . now that sure hits the spot! Danki, Rachel."

"You're welcome." Rachel decided to stay and watch the workers awhile. Suddenly, the ladder Uncle Amos stood on wobbled, and his hammer dropped to the ground with a thud.

Rachel rushed forward and reached for it. *Smack!*—she bumped heads with her oldest brother, Henry, who'd also reached for the hammer.

"Ouch!" Rachel and Henry said at the same time.

"Are you two okay?" Grandpa asked with a look of concern.

"I'm fine. It's just a little bump," Rachel said.

Henry nodded. "I'm okay, too." He looked at Rachel. "You shouldn't have tried to pick up that hammer."

"I was only trying to help." She rubbed her forehead.

"I was going to get it." Henry shook his head. "You shouldn't even be near the worksite, Rachel. Don't you realize this is men's work?"

Rachel clamped her teeth together. *The men and boys get to have all the fun,* she thought. *I wish I'd been a boy!*

Pap touched Rachel's shoulder. "Maybe you should go see if your *mamm* [mom] has something for you to do."

"That's right." Grandpa smiled at Rachel. "We'll see you at noon, when it's time for lunch."

With head down and shoulders slumped, Rachel headed up the driveway. *Oomph!*—she ran right into someone, spilling a can of nails all over the ground.

She looked up. Orlie Troyer, her friend from school, stared at her.

"Are you okay?" he asked.

She nodded. "I–I'm fine. I'll help you pick up the nails."

"Don't bother; I can manage." Orlie scooped up a handful of nails and tossed them back in the can. "What are you doing out here by the worksite, Rachel?"

"I took water to the men."

"Well, you'd better get back to the house before you get hurt. Working on the greenhouse is men's work."

"What would you know about that? You're not a man!" Before Orlie could respond, Rachel hurried away.

When she came to the pile of lumber, she paused. Some pieces didn't look so big. She figured she could probably carry a few of them to the worksite. Maybe then everyone would see that she could help with the greenhouse, too—even if she wasn't a man.

Rachel bent and picked up a piece of wood. "Ouch! Ouch!"

Tears filled her eyes as pain shot through her thumb. She let the wood fall to the ground and stared at her hand. An ugly splinter was stuck in her thumb!

Jacob rushed to her. "What are you yelling about, Rachel?"

She held out her hand. "I've got a nasty *schliffer* [splinter] in my thumb."

"How'd you do that?"

"I picked up a piece of wood to take to the worksite." Rachel's chin trembled as she struggled not to cry. She didn't want Jacob to call her a boppli. "I didn't know there'd be splinters in the lumber."

"It's wood, little *bensel* [silly child]. It's bound to have splinters." Jacob clicked his tongue, the way Mom often did. "You can help best by going to the house and helping Mom get our lunch ready."

"I will—after she takes the schliffer out of my finger." Sniffling and blinking, Rachel hurried to the house.

Rachel found her sister, Esther, as well as Mom, Grandma Yoder, and several other women, scurrying around the kitchen, making sandwiches.

Mom motioned to the refrigerator. "Good, you're just in time to help us with—" She stared at Rachel. "Have you been crying?"

Rachel nodded. "I—I had some trouble outside."

"What kind of trouble?" Esther asked.

"First I bumped heads with Henry when I was trying to pick up a hammer. Then I ran into Orlie and knocked a can of nails out of his hand." Rachel sniffed a couple of times. "Then I was going to carry some wood over to the worksite, but I ended up with this!" Rachel held up her throbbing thumb.

"*Ach* [Oh], that's a nasty looking schliffer," Mom said, clicking her tongue. "I'd better get that out for you."

Sniff! Sniff! "It's gonna hurt, isn't it?"

"Taking it out might hurt a little, but it will hurt much worse if the splinter stays in your thumb," Mom said.

Grandma nodded. "And if you don't take it out, it could get infected."

"Sit down and I'll take care of it." Mom went to the cupboard and returned with bandages, antiseptic, a pair of tweezers, and a needle from her sewing basket.

Rachel sank into a chair and closed her eyes. She hoped it wouldn't hurt too badly. She hoped she wouldn't start sobbing.

Esther held Rachel's hand and spoke soothing words while Mom dug out the splinter. "It's okay, Rachel. The schliffer will be out soon."

Rachel kept her eyes shut and struggled not to cry as Mom poked at the splinter with the needle.

"Got it!" Mom dabbed Rachel's thumb with some antiseptic and covered it with a bandage.

"Does that feel better?"

Rachel opened her eyes. "It still hurts a little, but not as much as it did before."

Grandma patted Rachel's shoulder. "You're a brave little girl."

Rachel liked hearing that she was brave, but she didn't like being called a little girl. She figured it was best not to tell that to Grandma, though.

"It's sure a warm day." Mom fanned herself with the corner of her apron.

"It is a bit *schtinkich* [stuffy] in here," Esther agreed.

"Why don't you two sit and rest awhile?" Grandma suggested. "Rachel and I can finish making the sandwiches. Isn't that right, Rachel?"

Rachel nodded. At least Grandma thought she was grown up enough to help with lunch. She glanced out the kitchen window and spotted Jacob and Orlie hauling more wood to the worksite. They walked slowly down the driveway. Rachel figured they were probably hot and tired.

I guess it is hard work. It might be more fun for me to watch the men build the greenhouse than try to help with it. Rachel smiled as she thought, *I can hardly wait to help Grandpa after the greenhouse is open for business!*

Chapter 2
A Trip to Town

The sun cast an orange tint into Rachel's room as she scrambled out of bed on Monday. Since school was out for the summer, Grandpa had promised to take Rachel to town with him. He was going to buy some things he needed for his new greenhouse. Rachel looked forward to spending the day with Grandpa.

Rachel raced to the closet, put on a clean dress, and rushed out the door. When she got to the bottom of the stairs, she stopped and sniffed. The sweet smell of cinnamon coming from the kitchen made her stomach rumble.

I'll bet Mom baked cinnamon rolls. Rachel smacked her lips in anticipation.

When she entered the kitchen, she was surprised to see just one bowl and a small plate on the table. Mom was the only one in the room.

"*Hoscht du schunn geese* [Have you already eaten]?" she asked when Mom turned from the sink, where she was washing dishes.

Mom nodded. "I ate with your *daed* [dad] and *brieder* [brothers] before they went to work in the fields."

"What about Grandpa?" Rachel asked. "Has he eaten, too?"

"Jah. He's in the barn getting his horse and buggy ready to go to town."

Rachel sighed. "I was afraid he might have left without me."

Mom pointed to the table. "You'd better hurry and eat your cereal and cinnamon roll."

Rachel scurried to the refrigerator and took out a carton of milk. She poured some into her bowl, then returned to the refrigerator and grabbed a pitcher of apple juice.

The juice sloshed in the pitcher as she bounded back across the room.

"*Dummel dich net* [Take your time, don't hurry]!" Mom said, shaking her head. "You have plenty of time. If you spill juice it'll make a sticky mess, and I just scrubbed the floor."

"Sorry, Mom. I want to eat quickly so I can go to town with Grandpa." Rachel poured a glass of juice and put the pitcher back in the refrigerator.

"That's fine, but wash your breakfast dishes before you go."

"I will." Rachel sat at the table and bowed her head for silent prayer. *Dear God: Danki for this day I get to spend with Grandpa. Bless this food to my body. Amen.*

"I'll leave the dishwater in the sink for you to use, and then I'm going outside to hang a few clothes on the line," Mom said when Rachel finished her prayer. "If I see your *grossdaadi* [grandfather], I'll tell him you're eating breakfast and will be out soon."

"Okay, Mom."

Rachel quickly ate her cinnamon roll. Then she drank the apple juice. "Mmm. . ." She smacked her lips. "This is so *gut* [good]. I think I'll have some more." She hurried to the refrigerator and poured another glass.

When she started back, she nearly dropped her glass. Cuddles sat on the table, lapping milk from Rachel's bowl of cereal!

Rachel clapped her hands, and the cat leaped off the table. "Shame on you, Cuddles! You know you're not supposed to be up there!"

Meow! Cuddles looked at Rachel as if to say, "I was hungry."

"Oh, all right." Rachel put the cereal on the floor beside the cat. "It's full of germs now anyway, so you may as well eat it!"

Lap. . .lap. . .lap. Cuddles slurped the milk with her little pink tongue. *Crunch. . .crunch. . .crunch.* She ate the rest of the cereal.

"What is that cat doing eating from your *schissel* [bowl]?" Mom hollered when she entered the kitchen.

Rachel gulped. "I–I'm sorry, Mom," she stammered. "I went to the refrigerator to get more juice, and when I turned around, Cuddles was on the table, eating my cereal."

"And just how did your cereal bowl get on the floor?" Mom asked.

"I—uh—figured since Cuddles had already eaten out of my bowl, and it was full of germs, I may as well let her eat the rest of it."

Mom frowned. "You know how I feel about animals eating from our dishes." She pointed to Cuddles. "Take her outside right now!"

Rachel picked up the cat and set her on the porch. "Now you be good," she said as Cuddles curled into a ball and began to purr.

"I'll wash my dishes now," Rachel said when she returned to the kitchen. She set the bowl, plate, and glass in the sink and plunged her hands into the soapy water.

"Cuddles probably got in when I went to hang my clothes on the line, so I know it wasn't your fault she was on the table." Mom peered at Rachel over the top of her glasses. "But I better never see that cat eating out of your dish again! If I do, you'll wash all the dishes after every meal for a whole week. Is that clear?"

"Jah, Mom," Rachel nodded. "I'll make sure it doesn't happen again."

A little later, as Rachel and Grandpa headed for town, the buggy hit a pothole in the road, nearly knocking Rachel out of her seat.

"Sorry about that," Grandpa said. "I didn't realize there was a rut or I would have avoided it."

Rachel looked at him and smiled. "It's okay, Grandpa. I'm enjoying the ride."

He grinned and patted her knee. "I like your positive attitude today, Rachel. It's always good to look on the bright side of things."

"Sometimes, when things don't go so well, it's hard for me to see the bright side," Rachel admitted.

Grandpa nodded. "That's when we need to

remember Psalm 32:11: 'Rejoice in the Lord and be glad.' We should try to rejoice no matter what happens—even in the middle of our troubles."

Rachel smiled and relaxed against the seat. She enjoyed listening to the steady *clip-clop, clip-clop* of the horse's hooves and watching all the cars zip past in the opposite lane. She dreamed about riding in a convertible some day, but she wondered if that dream would ever come true. She was sure it would be exciting to travel fast with the top of the car down and the wind in her face.

Beep! Beep! A horn honked as a car whipped around them.

A muscle on Grandpa's face quivered as he gripped the reins and guided the horse closer to the side of the road. "There's way too much traffic today," he mumbled. "I wish I'd picked a different day to go to town. Maybe we should have stayed home."

"You're not going back, I hope." Rachel had looked forward to spending the day with Grandpa. She'd be disappointed if he decided to go home.

Grandpa shook his head. "Don't worry. I won't go home until my errands are done. Fast cars just make me *naerfich* [nervous], and I don't like all this traffic."

Rachel didn't mind the traffic, and she thought

fast cars were exciting. She decided not to mention that, though. She didn't want to say anything that might spoil her day with Grandpa, so she decided to change the subject.

"Did you know my birthday's coming soon?" she asked.

"I think I may have heard something about that. Remind me now—how old will you be?"

"Eleven."

"Hmm. . ." Grandpa's lips twitched. "You've gotten so tall, I thought maybe you'd skipped a few years and had become a teenager."

Rachel giggled. "Are you teasing me?"

He nodded and chuckled. "You know me. . . . I do like to tease now and then."

She smiled. "That's one of the things I like about you, Grandpa. You're always so much fun to be with."

"I enjoy being with you, too." Grandpa looked at her and winked. "So what do you hope to get for your birthday?"

"I'd really like a trip to Hershey Park." Rachel sighed. "But I'm sure that won't happen."

"What makes you think so?"

"Because when I asked Pap about going he said he was too busy, and that Mom wasn't up to making the trip." She slowly shook her head. "I'll probably never go to Hershey Park, or anyplace else where there are fun rides."

"Never say never," Grandpa said. "Sometimes the things we want happen when we least expect them."

Hope rose inside Rachel. Maybe Mom and Pap would surprise her with a trip to Hershey Park for her birthday. Maybe Grandpa knew about it and was keeping it a secret.

"I don't know about you, but I'm getting hungry," Grandpa said when they had purchased flower pots, potting soil, gardening gloves, and packets of seeds. These were all things he would either use or sell in his greenhouse.

Rachel patted her stomach. "I'm hungry, too."

"I'll let you choose where we'll have our lunch," Grandpa said.

Rachel smiled. "I'd like to eat at the Bird-in-Hand Family Restaurant. They have real tasty food there."

"I like eating there, too," Grandpa said as he guided the horse and buggy onto the road.

When they entered the restaurant, Rachel's stomach rumbled and her nose twitched. The delicious aromas coming from the kitchen made her even hungrier.

The hostess showed them to a table. Then a waitress asked what they would like to drink.

"I'll have a glass of iced tea," Grandpa said. "How about you, Rachel?"

"I'd like a glass of milk."

"Do you know what you'd like to eat?" the waitress asked.

"I think I'll have the buffet." Grandpa smiled at Rachel. "Does that sound good to you?"

"That suits me fine." She licked her lips. "There are always lots of good things on the buffet, and they even have pickled beets on the salad bar!"

Grandpa chuckled. "You take after your mamm, Rachel. She's always liked pickled beets."

"Help yourself when you're ready," the waitress said. "I'll have your beverages at the table when you get back."

Rachel pushed her chair aside and scurried to the salad bar. She didn't care much for lettuce, but she liked some of the other vegetables there. So she loaded her plate and made sure she got plenty of pickled beets.

A girl with blond hair in a ponytail stepped up to Rachel and studied her a few seconds. "Is your name Rachel Yoder?"

"Yes," Rachel said.

"I thought so. We met at the farmer's market last summer." The girl tilted her head. "You look different than the last time I saw you. I don't think you wore glasses then."

"I got my glasses about a month ago." Rachel smiled at the girl. "Your name's Sherry, isn't it?"

"That's right."

"You had a cute dog with you. I remember we took it for a walk."

"Yes, we did. You should see how much Bundles has grown since then."

"My cat, Cuddles, has grown a lot, too— especially around the middle. I think it's because she eats so much," Rachel said.

"What are you doing here?" Sherry asked. "Are you going to the farmer's market?"

Rachel shook her head. "I came with my grandpa so he could buy some things for his new greenhouse."

"That sounds interesting."

"Yes, and I'm going to help him there when I'm not busy with other things," Rachel said. "What are you doing here?"

Sherry motioned to a woman sitting at a table across the room. "I came with my mother. We went shopping for a new quilt to put in our guest room."

"My mother made a quilt for my sister when she got married," Rachel said. "She used the Lone Star pattern."

"Will you help in your grandpa's greenhouse all summer?" Sherry asked. "Or will your family take a vacation?"

Rachel shook her head. "My mom's due to have a baby soon, so we won't go on vacation. How about you?"

"We may visit my aunt and uncle in California. My brother's planning to take me to Hershey Park sometime this summer, too."

Rachel couldn't help but feel envious. Hearing that Sherry was going to Hershey Park made her wish all the more that she could go there.

"It was nice to see you, Rachel." Sherry turned away from the salad bar. "Maybe I'll see you sometime later this summer."

Rachel smiled. "That would be nice."

When Sherry walked away, Rachel finished filling her plate and took it to the table where Grandpa waited. Despite longing for things she might never get to do, she was excited about the things they'd bought for Grandpa's greenhouse. And she was excited about helping him there. At least that was something to look forward to.

Chapter 3

Trouble by the Road

"The hurrier I go, the behinder I get," Grandpa mumbled as he hurried toward his greenhouse the following morning.

"I wish I could help you today," Rachel called from the garden, where she and Jacob were picking strawberries.

"Maybe you can help me later," Grandpa called as he kept walking.

Rachel dropped two berries into the basket by her knees. "I don't think there's much chance of that. When I'm done here, I'll have to spend the rest of the day selling these *aebier* [strawberries] from our roadside stand," she said as Grandpa disappeared.

"*Grummel net um mich rum* [Don't grumble around me]." Jacob tossed a berry, and it splattered on Rachel's arm.

"Stop! I'll end up with berry juice all over my dress!" Rachel grabbed a berry and threw it at Jacob. She laughed when it hit his nose.

"You'd better quit fooling around! You'll be in trouble if Mom sees you're playing."

"What about you?" Rachel frowned. "You threw an *aebeer* [strawberry] at me first."

"You didn't have to throw one back, little bensel."

"Stop calling me a silly child!" Rachel's fingers itched to pitch another berry at Jacob, but she heard the screen door open and saw Mom step onto the porch.

Plunk! Plunk! Plunk! Rachel dropped one strawberry after another into the basket. When Mom disappeared around the side of the house, Rachel popped a juicy berry into her mouth and giggled. "Mmm. . .this tastes *wunderbaar* [wonderful]."

"You'll never get enough berries picked to sell if you keep eating 'em," Jacob said, shaking his head.

"I only ate one." Rachel glared at Jacob. "And quit telling me what to do. You're not my boss."

"Someone has to tell you what to do when you're fooling around."

"I'm not fooling around." Rachel lifted her basket. "I have just as many berries as you do."

"Whatever you say, little bensel." Jacob snickered and moved to the next row.

That was fine with Rachel; she'd rather not work too close to her teasing brother.

She leaned over, plucked off another berry, and was about to put it in her basket, when—*Peck! Peck!*—their mean old goose nipped the back of Rachel's legs.

"Yeow!" Rachel dropped the berry and whirled around.

Honk! Honk! Honk! The goose flapped her wings and grabbed a berry in her beak.

Before Rachel could react, Jacob waved his hands and hollered, "Get away from here you stupid *gans* [goose]!"

The goose bobbed her head up and down, sounded another loud *Honk!* and waddled away.

Rachel sighed with relief. "Danki, Jacob. I thought that goose was gonna get me."

"I think she was after the strawberries and just wanted to get you out of her way," Jacob said. "She likes to sneak to the garden and help herself when no one's looking."

Rachel's hand trembled as she picked up the berry. "That gans is nothing but trouble. I wish Pap would get rid of her!"

"If she keeps getting into trouble, maybe he will." Jacob grabbed his box of berries. "I've filled eight boxes now, so I think I'll take 'em out to the stand. Are you ready to join me, or did you want to pick more?"

"I have eight boxes, too, so I'm gonna stop picking," Rachel said. "But before I come to the stand, I think I'll go inside and get some of my painted rocks to sell."

"I don't think anyone will want a *dumm* [dumb] old rock, but if you want to try selling some then suit yourself." Jacob gathered all the berries and put them in the wheelbarrow. "I'll see you at the stand!" He wheeled the boxes of berries down the driveway toward the roadside stand Pap had built.

Rachel hurried into the house, raced up the stairs, and opened her dresser drawer, where she kept several painted rocks. She found an empty box in her closet and put three ladybug rocks inside, along with two rocks she'd painted to look like turtles. She grunted when she picked up the box. The rocks sure made it heavy!

Huffing and puffing, Rachel stumbled down the stairs. When she stepped onto the back porch, she noticed Mom sitting in a chair, shelling peas.

"What are you doing, Rachel?" Mom asked. "I

thought you and Jacob were in the garden picking aebier."

Rachel's arms hurt, so she set the box of rocks on the small table by the door. "We were. Jacob took the strawberries out to the stand while I came to get some painted rocks to sell."

"That's a good idea, Rachel. I hope you sell them." Mom smiled. "I'll let you know when lunch is ready, and then you and Jacob can take turns coming up to the house to eat."

"Can't we eat lunch at the stand? I don't want to leave my rocks with Jacob. He might give them away."

Mom shook her head. "I don't think Jacob would do something like that, but if you'd like to eat at the stand, I'll bring lunch to you when it's ready."

"Danki." Rachel picked up the box and trudged down the stairs, panting as she made her way down the driveway.

"This is sure heavy," she said, placing the box on one end of the stand.

Jacob rolled his eyes. "I still think selling rocks is a dumm idea. I'll bet no one will even look at them."

"I bet they will."

"Bet they won't."

Rachel bit her lip. There was no point arguing about it. Jacob would see that he was wrong when she sold her first painted rock.

"Have you had any customers?" Rachel asked as she set the rocks on the other side of the strawberries.

He shook his head. "Only a couple of cars have passed, and no buggies at all."

Rachel shielded her eyes from the sun's glare. "It's still early. I'm sure someone will stop soon."

"I hope so because it's already hot and muggy, and I don't want to sit out here all day and sweat."

"Now who's grumbling?" Rachel nudged Jacob's arm with her elbow. "Huh?"

"I'm not grumbling, just stating facts." He wiped the sweat on his forehead with his shirtsleeve. "If it's this hot so early in the day, I can only imagine how it'll feel this afternoon."

Rachel sat on the folding chair beside Jacob. She glanced at the other side of the driveway, where Grandpa's greenhouse had been built. No cars or buggies were there, either. "It looks like we're not the only ones who don't have customers," she said. "Grandpa's greenhouse looks deserted."

Jacob nodded. "Everyone must either be at home, working, or shopping in town."

Rachel leaned on the wooden counter. "If you could be doing anything else right now, what would it be?"

"I'd be sitting on a big rock at the creek with my bare feet dangling in the water." Jacob looked over at Rachel. "What would you be doing?"

"The creek sounds nice, but I'd probably be in the greenhouse helping Grandpa." She sat up straight. "No, wait. I'd be on one of those wild rides at Hershey Park."

Jacob grunted. "I'd enjoy that, too, but it doesn't look like we'll go anywhere this summer. Not with so much work in the fields and the boppli coming soon."

Rachel sighed. "I wonder if I'll ever get to do anything fun."

Before Jacob could respond, Audra rode up on her scooter. It reminded Rachel of her skateboard. Unlike English scooters that sometimes had engines, Audra's Amish scooter was similar to a skateboard with handles.

"*Wie geht's* [How are you]?" Audra asked, smiling at Rachel.

"Okay. How about you?"

"I'm doing good." Audra stepped down from the scooter and leaned on the counter. "I came to see if you could play."

"I can't today. Jacob and I have to sit here and try to sell these aebier." Rachel motioned to the box of berries sitting closest to her. "Would you like to buy some?"

"Sorry, but I don't have any money with me." Audra looked up at the yard. "Can't you leave the stand for a while? I was hoping we could jump on your trampoline."

"I wish I could, but I'll be in trouble with Mom if I don't try to sell these berries."

"Should I come back later this afternoon?" Audra asked. "Maybe you'll be free to play then."

Rachel shook her head. "If the berries sell, I'll help Grandpa in his new greenhouse this afternoon. If they don't sell, I'll probably be stuck here in the hot sun for the rest of the day."

"*Die Rachel is die ganz zeit am grumble* [Rachel is grumbling all the time]," Jacob said to Audra.

Rachel nudged him. "That's not true. Besides, you grumbled about how hot it is. Remember?"

"Jah, but I don't grumble all the time. You always grumble about something."

"Do not."

"Do so."

"Do not."

"Do so."

"I'd better go," Audra said. "*She dich, eich, wider* [See you later]!" She waved at Rachel and glided away.

Rachel looked over at Jacob. "I wonder why Audra doesn't have to work today. It doesn't seem fair, does it?"

"You're grumbling again."

"Am not. I'm just stating facts."

"Oh, good, I think a customer's coming." Jacob motioned to a car coming down the road. But instead of stopping, it sped up and passed the stand. A small rock from the road hurled through the air. It hit the front of the stand, putting a hole through the letter *S* in the "Strawberries for Sale" sign Jacob had painted and nailed to the stand.

"That's great!" Jacob mumbled. "Now our sign says 'trawberries for Sale." He looked at Rachel and shook his head. "Who's ever heard of trawberries, and who's gonna stop at a stand selling some weird kind of berry?"

Rachel poked Jacob. "I guess you think you're funny, huh?"

Jacob laughed. "Jah, I'm the man selling strawberries with a great sense of humor."

Rachel grunted. "You're not a man!"

"I will be soon."

A car pulled into the driveway, and a bald, middle-aged man got out of the car. He walked to the stand and pointed at the strawberries. "How much are you asking?"

"One dollar a box," Rachel said.

"I'll take two boxes." The man motioned to Grandpa's greenhouse. "I'm going to look at some plants. Would you please put the strawberries on the front seat of my car while I'm gone?" He hurried away before Rachel could respond.

"That was rude," Jacob said. "He didn't even pay for the berries."

"Maybe he'll pay for them when he's done at the greenhouse." Rachel picked up two boxes of berries and took them to the man's car. She opened the door on the driver's side and placed them on the seat. Then she closed the door and raced back to the stand.

"I'm thirsty," Jacob said. "I think I'll run up to the house and get something cold to drink."

"That sounds good. Could you get something for me, too?"

"Jah, sure." Jacob scurried up the driveway.

The man finally returned to his car, but instead of coming to the stand to pay for the berries, he jumped into his car and started to drive away.

Suddenly, he slammed on the brakes and climbed out of the car. He stomped to the stand and shook his finger at Rachel. "Did you put those berries on the front seat of my car?"

"Yes," she admitted.

"Just look what you've done!" He whirled around.

Rachel gasped. Bright red berry juice covered the man's tan-colored pants!

"I—I only set them there because you told me to," she said in a shaky voice.

"I did tell you to put them on the seat, but I didn't think you'd put them where I would sit on them!" A muscle of the side of the man's neck quivered, and his pale eyebrows pulled together.

"I–I'm sorry. I thought you'd come back to the stand to pay for the strawberries, and I was gonna tell you then that the berries were in the front seat of your car." She drew in a quick breath. "But you didn't come back."

"Oh, you're right, I should have paid for the berries, and I did tell you to put them in my front seat. So I guess it's more my fault than yours." The man reached into his pants pocket and handed Rachel four dollars. "The berries in my car are too smashed to eat, but here's enough money for two more boxes, plus the ones I sat on."

Rachel shook her head. "You don't have to pay for the ones that are ruined."

He placed the money on the counter and picked up two boxes of berries. "I'll pay for all four boxes. Maybe my wife can make jelly out of the squished ones."

Rachel smiled. "Thank you."

"You're welcome." The man hurried back to his car and drove away just as a horse and buggy pulled in. It was Rachel's aunt Karen and her little boy, Gerald.

"Wie geht's?" Aunt Karen asked, walking to the stand.

"I'm doing okay," Rachel said. "How about you?"

"Gerald and I are well." Aunt Karen patted Gerald's head. "We were on our way home from town and noticed you, so I decided to stop and see what you have for sale."

"Jacob and I are selling strawberries." Rachel motioned to her painted rocks. "And these."

"Those are nice. Did you paint them yourself?" Aunt Karen asked.

Rachel nodded. "Painting rocks is a hobby of mine."

Gerald eyed a turtle rock; then he tugged his mother's skirt and said, "*Shillgrott* [Turtle]. *Geb's mir* [Give it to me]!"

Aunt Karen shook her head. "That's no way to ask for something. You must say *sei so gut* [please]."

Gerald looked at his mother with pleading eyes. "Sei so gut?"

Aunt Karen squeezed his shoulder. "Jah, you may have the turtle." She opened her purse. "How much are the rocks, Rachel?"

"I'm asking a dollar for them, but since Gerald's my cousin, he can have one for free," Rachel said.

Aunt Karen shook her head. "You worked hard to paint these nice rocks, and I will pay."

"Danki," Rachel said as she took the dollar Aunt Karen handed her. "Would you like a box of strawberries, too?"

"I have a big strawberry patch in my garden, so I really don't need anymore." Aunt Karen smiled. "Your berries are nice and plump, so I'm sure you'll sell them in no time."

"I hope so, because I don't want to spend the whole day out here in the hot sun."

"It is quite warm," Aunt Karen agreed. She handed Gerald his turtle rock. "We'd best be on our way home now. Tell your mamm I said hello."

"I will," Rachel called as Aunt Karen and Gerald walked away.

Their buggy had just pulled out of the driveway when Jacob returned.

"I brought some of Pap's cold root beer," he said, handing Rachel a mug.

Rachel smiled. "Danki. It looks good."

Jacob took a big drink from his mug. "This sure hits the spot." He ran his tongue across his upper lip, where some foamy root beer had gathered.

Rachel laughed and sipped from her mug. "You're right; this does hit the spot! Pap makes the best root beer!"

Jacob glanced at the strawberries. "Looks like you sold two more boxes of berries while I was gone."

"Jah." Rachel told Jacob how the man had bought two more boxes of berries after he'd sat on the ones she'd put in his car. "I really felt bad about the man's berry pants," she added.

"That was a dumb thing to do, Rachel."

"The man said it was as much his fault because he told me to put the berries on the front seat."

Jacob shrugged. "I guess it was partly his fault then."

"Then Aunt Karen and Gerald came by." Rachel pointed to the spot where the painted turtle rock had been sitting. "She bought one of my rocks for Gerald."

"Really?"

"Jah. I told you I'd sell some rocks today."

"Puh!" Jacob flapped his hand like he was swatting a fly. "You've only sold one, and to a member of our family. I'd be more impressed if you'd sold the whole lot of them to a stranger."

Rachel frowned. "You don't have to be so mean."

"I wasn't being mean; I was just stating facts." He gulped more root beer. "Selling a rock to a relative doesn't count."

"Jah, it does."

"Does not."

"Does too, and I think you ought to stop—"

Woof! Woof! Jacob's dog, Buddy, bounded up to the stand and licked Rachel's arm with his big pink tongue.

"Get away from me!" Rachel pushed Buddy down. "Your breath is awful!"

Thunk!—Buddy's tail hit a berry box, knocking it to the ground.

"Oh, no," Rachel moaned. "Now the berries are dirty!" She bent over and was about to pick them up, when—*thunk!*—Buddy whacked another box with his tail.

Rachel glared at Jacob. "Look what your hairy

mutt's done! He's always causing trouble! Why's he out of his dog run?"

Jacob shrugged. "I don't know, but I'll put him back right away." He reached for Buddy's collar, but the dog put his paws in Rachel's lap and licked her face.

"Yuck! Go away, you hairy beast!"

Buddy grunted and flopped down on the berries he'd knocked to the ground.

Rachel groaned. "Trouble. . .trouble. . .Buddy's always causing trouble!" She pointed at Jacob. "You'd better pick some more berries!"

Jacob frowned. "Why me?"

"Because your *hund* [dog] knocked over the berries and squished them with his big hairy body. So you should be the one to pick more berries!"

"Oh, okay. It'll be better than sitting here listening to you grumble." Jacob scooped up the berry boxes and led Buddy up the driveway, mumbling, "Stupid *hund*!"

Rachel leaned on the counter and closed her eyes. She hoped the whole summer wouldn't be full of trouble.

Chapter 4

Camping Surprise

When Rachel stepped onto the porch the next morning, she spotted Cuddles lying on her back, playing with a piece of string.

"You're getting fat! You must be eating too many mice." Rachel scratched the cat's bulging belly. "Maybe I should cut back on your food."

Meow! Cuddles looked up at Rachel as if to say, "You'd better not!"

Rachel continued to rub the cat's belly. "Oh, don't worry; I promise I won't let you starve."

Cuddles closed her eyes and purred.

Rachel closed her eyes, too. It felt good to sit on the porch in a patch of warm sun. She wished she could stay here and pet Cuddles all day, but she had chores to do.

"I'm going to the chicken coop to feed the chickens. When I get back I'll give you some food," Rachel said, giving the cat's stomach one final rub.

When Rachel entered the chicken coop, she was relieved that the big red rooster wasn't there. She figured he must be outside hunting for bugs, taking a dirt bath, or chasing the smaller roosters around the yard. Whenever Rachel went into the coop and the big rooster was there, he usually caused trouble. Maybe she would have an easier time feeding the chickens today.

Rachel opened a can of chicken feed and poured some into the dishes. *Bawk! Bawk! Bawk!* A dozen red hens crowded around the dish, pecking at each other and gobbling up the food.

"There's plenty for everyone, so don't be in such a hurry," Rachel scolded. "If you eat too much you'll get fat like Cuddles."

Bawk! Bawk! The chickens continued to peck one another, eating as if this was their last meal.

Rachel took the watering dishes outside to fill.

"Rachel, check for eggs while you're in the coop," Mom called from the back porch.

Rachel cupped her hands around her mouth. "I will, Mom!"

Rachel rinsed the watering dishes and filled them with fresh water; then she carried them back to the coop. While the hens continued to eat and drink, she checked for eggs.

When she returned to the house, she found Mom in the kitchen, frying bacon.

"I got six eggs," Rachel said.

"That's good." Mom turned from the stove and smiled. "Would you please wash them and put them in the refrigerator?"

Rachel went to the sink and turned on the water. "I still need to feed Cuddles, but I'm not gonna give her as much food as normal."

"Why not?" Mom asked.

"She's getting fat. She looks like she's eaten too many *meis* [mice]. I think she needs to go on a diet."

Mom clicked her tongue. "Cuddles doesn't need to lose weight, Rachel. She's in a family way."

Rachel's mouth dropped open. "Cuddles is going to have *busslin* [kittens]?"

"That's right. I thought you knew."

Rachel shook her head. "I thought she'd been eating too much."

"No, she's going to have a batch of kittens. I'm guessing it will be soon."

"Oh, that's wunderbaar!" Rachel was so excited, she felt like doing a little dance. "I hope she has a whole bunch of busslin!"

Mom held up her hand. "Now don't get too excited. No matter how many kittens she has, you can't keep them. You'll need to find each of them a good home."

"Can't I keep just one?"

"Well, maybe. We'll have to wait and see." Mom turned back to the stove. "Oh, and Rachel, you'd better find a box in the barn and fill it with shredded newspaper. That way, Cuddles will have a nice, safe place to have her kittens." She pointed to the stack of newspapers inside the woodbox. "You can use some of those. We don't want Cuddles to have her babies in some strange place we don't know about."

"I'll fix it right after breakfast." Rachel could hardly wait until the kittens were born!

For the next several days Rachel closely watched Cuddles. She'd taken her into the barn and shown her the box she'd prepared. Cuddles didn't show much interest in the box. She just slept on the porch, while her stomach grew bigger.

"I saw Audra's mamm at the grocery store yesterday," Mom said to Rachel during breakfast on Thursday morning. "She said Audra would like you to spend Friday night with her."

"At her house?" Rachel asked.

Mom nodded.

"Couldn't Audra come over here? I don't want to leave Cuddles."

"Why not?"

Rachel reached for a piece of toast and slathered it with creamy peanut butter. "What if she has her *bopplin* [babies] while I'm gone? I should be here for that."

Jacob, who sat beside Rachel, grunted and nudged her arm. "The cat doesn't need you. She'll do just fine on her own."

"I understand why Rachel would want to be with Cuddles," Grandpa said. "I remember when I was a boy and my dog was expecting pups." He had a faraway look in his eyes. "I made sure I was there when Cindy's pups were born."

Mom patted Rachel's hand. "If it's all right with Audra's mamm, Audra can spend the night here."

"Oh, good. Can I walk over there after breakfast and ask her?" Rachel asked.

"Jah, but not until all your chores are done," Pap said.

Rachel nodded.

"This is so exciting!" Audra said as she and

Rachel entered the tent Pap set up for them in the backyard on Friday evening. "It's just like going camping; only we're not in the woods."

Rachel nodded. "It should be lots of fun."

Rachel was about to crawl into her sleeping bag when Audra hollered, "Wait! You'd better not get in!"

"Look! There's a big lump in there!"

Rachel studied her sleeping bag. Something was at the bottom of it! "Maybe it's a *maus* [mouse]," she said.

Audra covered her mouth and squealed. "Ach, I hope not! I don't like mice!"

"If it is a *maus*, I'd better let it out." Rachel unzipped the sleeping bag and pulled it open. "*Was in der welt* [What in all the world]?" She slowly shook her head.

"Wh–what is it?" Audra's voice trembled as she darted for the tent door.

"Look, it's Cuddles. She had her busslin inside my sleeping bag!"

Audra crept back in and peered inside the sleeping bag. "You're right!" Her eyes widened. "How many kittens do you think she has?"

Rachel studied the kittens. "I think I see six, but it's hard to tell for sure." She touched Audra's arm. "Aren't they tiny?"

Audra nodded. "Are you gonna leave them in the sleeping bag?"

"I don't know. I think I'd better get Pap." Rachel jumped up. "He'll know what to do!"

Rachel and Audra scurried out of the tent. "Pap, come quick!" Rachel shouted as they ran into the house.

Pap, who was sitting beside Mom on the living room sofa, looked up from the newspaper he was reading and frowned. "What are you yelling about, Rachel? I thought you and Audra had gone to bed."

"Cuddles had her busslin inside my sleeping bag!" Rachel dashed to the sofa. "Should I move them to the barn, Pap? Or leave them in the bag?"

"I'll see about moving them tomorrow," Pap said. "For tonight, I think it's best that you and Audra sleep in your nice clean bed and let Cuddles alone with her kittens."

"But what about our campout?" Rachel was glad the kittens had been born, but she was disappointed that she and Audra couldn't sleep in the tent. "Audra and I were going to pretend we were camping in the woods. It was gonna be lots of fun."

"You can have your backyard campout some

other time," Mom said. "Since your cat chose your sleeping bag to have her kittens in, you won't be able to sleep in it until it's been washed."

"Okay, Mom." Rachel grabbed Audra's hand. "Let's go to my room. We can pretend we're camping there."

Audra followed Rachel up the stairs. "I don't see how we can pretend we're camping when we have no tent," she said when they entered Rachel's room.

Rachel pointed to her bed. "We can sleep under there."

Audra frowned. "You want to sleep on the floor under your bed?"

Rachel nodded. "One time, before my cousin Mary moved to Indiana, she and I slept under my bed because a bat got into the room and we were scared."

Audra shivered. "I hope no bat gets in your room tonight. I'd really be scared!"

Rachel shook her head. "That won't happen because the window's closed." She grabbed a quilt and two pillows, shoved them under the bed, and crawled in behind them. "Are you coming?" she called to Audra.

Audra finally crawled in beside Rachel.

Rachel pulled the quilt around them and laid her head on a pillow.

"I didn't get as good a look at the busslin as I wanted to," Audra said, "but they looked like cute little things. Didn't you think so?"

"Jah, but I think all baby animals are cute." Rachel looked over at Audra. "Would you like to have a kitten when they're old enough to leave their mamm?"

"That would be nice. I'll have to ask my folks first, though." Audra yawned. "I'm awful sleepy all of a sudden. *Gut nacht* [Good night], Rachel."

"Gut nacht, Audra." Rachel closed her eyes. Soon she was fast asleep, dreaming of campfires, toasted marshmallows, and cuddly kittens.

When Rachel awoke the following day, she forgot where she was, and—*whack!*—she bumped her head on the bed when she tried to sit up. "Ouch, that hurt!" Then she remembered that she and Audra had pretended they were camping last night and slept under her bed.

Rachel glanced at Audra. "Wake up sleepyhead," she said, poking Audra's arm.

Audra yawned and stretched her arms across the floor. "What time is it?"

"I don't know, but there's a ray of sun streaming

through a hole in my window shade," Rachel said. "Don't sit up straight or you might bump your head like I did."

"I'll be careful. Now let's hurry and get dressed so we can go see the kittens," Audra said as the girls crawled out from under the bed.

"That's a good idea." Rachel rubbed her lower back. "That floor was sure hard. I think we should have slept in the bed instead of under it."

Audra nodded. "My back feels sore, too."

"I'm sure we'll feel better when we move around," Rachel said. "At least that's what Grandpa always says after he's been sitting awhile."

Audra laughed. "When my daed comes home after working at the blacksmith shop all day he says he feels better after he lies down."

"Pap says that after he's worked in the fields, too." Rachel went to her closet and took out a clean dress. "If Mom hasn't started breakfast yet, we can go outside and check on the kittens right away."

"I still can't believe Cuddles had her busslin inside your sleeping bag," Audra said.

"I guess she was looking for a place that was nice and soft." Rachel grabbed Audra's hand. "Let's hurry downstairs, *schnell* [quickly]!"

When they entered the kitchen, Rachel was glad to see that Mom wasn't there. If she had been, she would have expected Rachel to help with breakfast.

Rachel opened the back door and stepped onto the porch. Audra followed. They entered the tent, and Rachel pulled her sleeping bag open. She was surprised to see that it was empty.

Audra frowned. "What happened to Cuddles and her kittens?"

"I don't know. She might have moved them, or maybe Pap took them to the barn."

"Let's go see!"

The girls raced across the yard and into the barn. Pap and Henry were there, feeding the horses.

"Cuddles and her busslin aren't in my sleeping bag!" Rachel said as she stepped up to Pap. "Do you know where they are?"

He motioned to the wooden box Rachel had made for Cuddles. "I put them in there."

Rachel and Audra dashed across the room and skidded to a stop in front of the box.

"Oh, just look at them! There's six busslin, just like I thought." Rachel grinned at Audra. "Aren't they the cutest little things you've ever seen?"

"They sure are." Audra pointed to a gray and white one that looked just like Cuddles. "If my mamm says it's all right, I'd like to have that one when it's big enough."

Rachel nodded. "If you get to have one of Cuddles' kittens, whenever we get together to play our cats can play, too."

"My birthday's in six weeks," Audra said. "Do you think the kitten will be ready to leave Cuddles by then?"

"I'm sure it will, and it would make a great birthday present." Rachel squeezed Audra's arm. "Speaking of birthdays, my birthday's next Friday, and Pap said he might take our family out for supper that night. Maybe he'll let you go along."

"I'd like that very much," Audra said with a nod.

"I'll be right back!" Rachel raced over to Pap. "Can Audra go with us when we eat out for my birthday?"

Pap smiled. "I don't see why not. Of course, she'll have to get her parents' permission."

"All right!" Rachel clapped her hands, spun around in a circle, and raced back to Audra. "Pap said you can join us!"

Audra smiled. "Would you like anything special for your birthday?"

"You don't have to bring me a present," Rachel said.

"I want to." Audra hugged Rachel. "You're my best friend, and best friends always give each other something for their birthday."

"I'm sure I'll like whatever you give me." Rachel could hardly wait until Friday!

Chapter 5

A Birthday Surprise

When Rachel woke on Friday morning, one week later, she threw back the covers, leaped out of bed, and quickly dressed. Today was her eleventh birthday! She could hardly wait to see what surprises waited for her downstairs!

When Rachel entered the kitchen there was no sign of Mom. None of the usual good smells came from the kitchen, either. That was strange.

She glanced around. No birthday presents waited on the counter or the table. That wasn't a good sign.

She looked at the clock above the refrigerator. It was seven a.m. Surely Mom must be up by now.

Rachel hurried to her parents' bedroom and nearly bumped into Grandpa as he stepped out of his room. "I'm glad to see you're up, Rachel," he said. "Your mamm asked me to give you a message."

"What?"

"She's in labor, and your daed hired a driver to take them to the hospital." Grandpa squeezed Rachel's shoulder. "Soon you'll be a big sister. Isn't that exciting?"

Rachel's mouth dropped open. "Mom's having the boppli today?"

Grandpa nodded. "It seems so."

"B—but she can't have it today." Rachel's lip quivered. "Today's my birthday. Pap's supposed to take us out for supper tonight. Audra's planning to go with us."

"Babies don't wait, Rachel, and your mamm certainly won't go anywhere this evening. We'll have to celebrate your birthday some other night. Oh, and I ordered a birthday present for you, but it hasn't come in yet." Grandpa hugged Rachel. "*Hallich gebottsdaag* [Happy birthday], Rachel. What a great birthday present you'll get! Your baby schweschder or bruder."

Rachel swallowed around the lump that had formed in her throat. She wasn't sure she wanted a baby sister or brother. And she sure didn't want the baby to be born on her birthday!

"I'm going out to the phone shed to check the answering machine," Grandpa said. "When your daed calls to tell us the boppli's been born, we'll go to the hospital to meet the new baby." He patted Rachel's head. "Would you like that?"

She nodded slowly. "I—I guess so."

"While I'm in the phone shed would you like me to phone the Burkholders and let Audra know we won't go to supper tonight?"

"I—I guess she does need to know." The lump in Rachel's throat tightened. What a disappointing day!

"I haven't had breakfast yet, and neither has Jacob or Henry," Grandpa said. "Would you fix us all something to eat?"

"Okay, Grandpa." Rachel trudged off to the kitchen. She would fix breakfast for Grandpa and her brothers, but she didn't think she'd be able to eat. Her birthday was ruined, and the only surprise was that Mom was at the hospital having a baby.

"Why don't you eat your oatmeal?" Jacob asked Rachel as they sat at the table with Grandpa and Henry.

Rachel shrugged. "I'm not hungry."

"You'd better eat or you won't have the strength to do your chores," Henry said.

Grandpa looked at Rachel and raised his

eyebrows. "Your bruder's right; you do need to eat."

"Maybe I'll have a piece of toast," she mumbled.

"Have you checked the answering machine?" Jacob asked Grandpa.

He nodded. "I went to the phone shed right before breakfast, but there wasn't a message from your daed yet. I'll check again after we eat."

Jacob nudged Rachel. "How come my oatmeal doesn't have any raisins? Mom always fixes it with raisins."

Rachel glared at him. "You should be glad I fixed your breakfast at all—especially since today's my birthday!"

"Oh, that's right," Henry said. "Hallich gebottsdaag, Rachel."

"Jah, happy birthday," Jacob mumbled, oatmeal filling his mouth.

Rachel frowned. Was that all she would get—a mumbled happy birthday? *I wonder how Jacob would like it if today was his birthday and no one cared.*

She pushed away from the table, biting her bottom lip so she wouldn't cry. "I'll get you some raisins!"

"Danki," Jacob said.

Rachel opened the cupboard where Mom kept

her baking supplies. She didn't see any raisins. She opened another cupboard. Still no raisins.

"Can't you find the box of raisins?" Jacob called over his shoulder.

"*Des kann ich finne* [I can find it]," Rachel said.

"Are you sure? Do you need me to help look for it?"

"Just stay where you are! I don't need your help!"

Grandpa turned and looked sternly at Rachel. "You don't have to be so snappish. Jacob was only offering to help."

"Sorry," Rachel mumbled as she choked back tears. It didn't seem fair that Grandpa was taking Jacob's side. Nothing about today seemed fair!

Rachel rummaged through a couple more cupboards and finally found the raisins next to a box of crackers. Someone must have put them there by mistake.

She plunked the box of raisins in front of Jacob. "Here you go!"

"Don't need 'em now." Jacob pointed to his empty bowl. "I finished my oatmeal."

Rachel clamped her teeth together. She knew if she told Jacob what she thought she'd get a lecture from Grandpa. She put the box of raisins back in the cupboard. Then she sat at the table and forced herself to eat a piece of toast.

When everyone had finished their breakfast and the men had gone outside, Rachel cleared the table and washed the dishes. She'd just dried the last dish when Grandpa stepped into the kitchen wearing a huge smile.

"Your daed called," he said.

"What'd he say? Has Mom had the boppli?"

He nodded. "They won't come home from the hospital until tomorrow, so we'll go over there today and meet your little sister."

Rachel dropped the dishtowel. "A baby girl?"

"Jah. I guess we'll find out what they've named her when we get to the hospital."

Rachel drew in a deep breath. She hadn't even thought about the baby needing a name. She wondered what name Mom and Pap would call her little sister. She wondered what the baby looked like. She wondered what it would be like having a baby in the house.

Rachel stared at the scenery as she sat in the back of Harold Johnson's van. She and Grandpa were on their way to the hospital. Jacob and Henry had stayed home because they had so much work to do. Esther and Rudy had gone to the farmer's market in Ephrata, so they didn't even know the baby had arrived. They were supposed to be back in time to join Rachel's family for her birthday supper and didn't know it had been cancelled.

Zip! Zip! Zip! Rachel placed her hand on her stomach. She felt like a zillion butterflies were zipping around in there. She was anxious to meet her baby sister, but she was also nervous. She hadn't felt this anxious since the day she'd gone to the eye doctor and found out she had to wear glasses.

"We're here," Harold announced. "Do you know how long you'll be?" he asked Grandpa.

"No more than an hour, I'm sure," Grandpa replied. "We don't want to tire my daughter and her wee one."

"That should work out fine," Harold said. "I have a few errands to run, but I'll be back in plenty of time to pick you up."

"Thank you." Grandpa opened the door for Rachel, and she stepped out of the van.

"Are you as excited as I am?" he asked as they entered the hospital.

"Jah." Her voice squeaked, and she swallowed a couple of times. She was really more nervous than excited.

"Your daed said your mamm's room is number

322, so we'll have to ride the elevator to the third floor."

When they stepped into the elevator, the butterflies in Rachel's stomach started zipping around again. What if she didn't like the baby? What if Mom and Pap liked the baby more than they liked her? Rachel had been the baby in their family for eleven years. Now she was not the youngest child anymore.

As they headed toward Mom's room, Rachel's heart hammered.

"Here we are," Grandpa said. "Room 322!" He pushed the door open, but Rachel hesitated. "Go on in," he said. "I'm right behind you."

Rachel entered the room and saw Mom lying in a bed. She held a baby in her arms. Pap sat beside the bed wearing a huge smile.

"Wie geht's?" Grandpa asked Mom.

"I'm a little tired, but doing fine."

Rachel stood to one side, unsure of what to say or do.

Mom smiled and motioned to Rachel. "*Kumme* [Come]. Kumme see your little schweschder."

Rachel moved to the bed and peered at the baby in Mom's arms. She had blond hair, the same color as Rachel's, and her little nose was turned up, the same as Jacob's.

"What do you think of our little Hannah?" Pap asked. "Isn't she a *schee* [pretty] boppli?"

Rachel nodded. She had to admit, Hannah was kind of pretty. "Why did you name her Hannah?" she asked.

"Because it was my mamm's name," Mom said. She looked at Grandpa and smiled. "We thought you might like having a granddaughter with the same name as Mama."

"Hannah's a very nice name; I'm glad you chose it." Tears welled in Grandpa's eyes. "Daughter, you do have a very schee boppli," he said, taking Mom's hand. "I only wish your mamm was here to meet her namesake."

Mom nodded and reached under her glasses to wipe away her own tears. "I wish that, too, but I'm grateful Mama's in heaven. I'm also happy you'll get to know our little Hannah." She smiled at Rachel again. "Where's Henry and Jacob? I want them to meet their baby sister, too."

"They're still working," Grandpa said. "They said to tell you that they're excited about the boppli and will see her when you bring her home tomorrow."

Mom nodded. "There's a lot of work to be done

on the farm, and with Levi here at the hospital, it's good that our boys are such hard workers."

Pap nodded. "I called Rudy and Esther and left a message after the boppli was born, so I expect they'll be here soon."

Rachel shook her head. "They were planning to go to the farmer's market in Ephrata today, remember?"

"Oh, that's right." Pap stroked the baby's head. "I guess they'll have to meet Hannah when we take her home tomorrow."

Mom motioned to the empty chair on the other side of her bed. "Rachel, would you like to sit down and hold your baby sister?"

Rachel swallowed hard. "I–I'm not sure I should."

"Why not?" asked Pap.

"She might cry or wet her *windel* [diaper]."

"She's sound asleep, so I'm sure she won't cry. And I just changed her before you got here, so you shouldn't have to worry about that, either," Mom said.

"Oh, okay." Rachel took a seat, and Pap placed the baby in her arms. Weren't Mom and Pap going to say anything about Rachel's birthday? Didn't they care that she'd missed her birthday dinner because of Hannah being born?

Pap placed his hand on Rachel's shoulder. "Since Hannah chose today to be born, the two of you will always share the same birthday," he said.

Rachel was glad Pap hadn't forgotten, but did he have to mention that she and Hannah would share the same birthday? And he still hadn't said a word about them not going to supper tonight, or even mentioned whether he and Mom had bought Rachel a present.

"Did you hear what I said about you and Hannah sharing a birthday?" Pap asked, nudging Rachel's arm.

Rachel nodded. She couldn't tell Mom or Pap that she didn't like the idea of sharing a birthday with Hannah.

As Mom took a nap and Pap and Grandpa talked about crops, Rachel thought about her birthday.

Wait! She suddenly thought. Henry and Jacob stayed home. *Maybe they're not working in the fields. Maybe they're planning something special for my birthday!*

Last year they had surprised her with a skateboard. Maybe they were making something for her. Or maybe Esther and Rudy had returned from the farmer's market and were helping them make a special dinner at home. The more Rachel thought about it, the more sure she became that the rest of her family was preparing to surprise her.

Awhile later, Rachel eagerly climbed into Harold Johnson's van. She barely noticed the other cars on the road or the scenery whizzing by. She was too busy wondering what her brothers might have planned.

"I'm glad to see you looking happier than you were earlier," Grandpa said to her as they rode along. "I thought you would enjoy seeing the boppli."

"Jah," Rachel said absently.

Finally, Harold's van pulled up to Rachel's house. While Grandpa paid Harold, Rachel dashed into the house, expecting to smell Esther's tasty dinner. "Hello! We're home!" she called as she banged the door behind her.

Silence answered her call. No pleasant aromas of her favorite dinner greeted her. She looked around the empty house.

"Well, Rachel," Grandpa said as he came through the door. "Your brothers will be in from the fields soon. They'll be hungry and tired. I guess it's up to you to find something for us all to eat." Grandpa walked into his room and closed his door.

Rachel bit her lip as she walked into the kitchen. Tears stung her eyes as she realized that none of her birthday dreams were going to come true. She sighed and opened the refrigerator door to figure out what to make for dinner. *Looks like the boppli will bring even more trouble into my life!*

Chapter 6

Trouble in the Greenhouse

The next morning, as Rachel had begun to wash the breakfast dishes, she saw Harold Johnson's van pull into the yard. "Harold's here," she said to Pap, who was sitting at the table drinking a second cup of coffee.

Pap jumped up and looked out the window. "I hired him to take me to Lancaster this morning."

"Does that mean you won't work today?" Rachel asked.

"That's right. I'm going to the hospital to see your mamm and sister. Henry and Jacob will work alone in the fields again today, but I'll help them tomorrow."

"Are Mom and the boppli coming home today?" Rachel asked.

"Jah, but probably not until later this afternoon."

"Then why are you leaving so early?"

"Because Harold has a dental appointment and several errands to run in Lancaster. So he's taking me to the hospital this morning. Hopefully, by the time he's done with everything, your mamm and Hannah will be ready to come home." Pap grabbed his straw hat from the wall peg near the door. "I'm heading out now, Rachel. Have a good day."

"Can I go?" she asked.

He shook his head. "No. Someone needs to be here to fix lunch for Grandpa, Henry, and Jacob, and I'm afraid that has to be you."

Rachel frowned. "Can't they fix their own lunches?"

"I'm sure they could, but since Grandpa will be busy in his greenhouse all day and your brothers are working, it makes sense that you fix lunch for everyone."

"But I wanted to help Grandpa today," Rachel whined. "He said I could help him this summer, and I haven't been there very much at all."

"You can go to the greenhouse after doing the breakfast dishes. I also want you to make sure the house is clean before we get home. Your mamm will feel good to see a clean house when she returns." Pap smiled and headed out the door.

Rachel dropped her sponge into the soapy water. Several bubbles floated up and hit the ceiling. "Work, work, work. All I ever do is work," she grumbled. "I wish I could spend the day at the creek or helping Grandpa. Summer's half over and I haven't done anything fun. I didn't even have fun on my birthday!"

Rachel sloshed the sponge against a dirty plate as she continued to grumble. "After I finish these dishes, I'll clean the house quickly so I can go to the greenhouse. That will be a lot more fun than doing dishes or cleaning house!"

Rachel's bare toes tingled as she raced through the grass toward Grandpa's greenhouse that afternoon. She loved going barefooted during summer months. She especially liked dangling her feet in the cool creek, but she probably wouldn't have time for that today. When she finished helping Grandpa, she'd have to start supper and then clean more dishes.

When Rachel entered the greenhouse, she found Grandpa sitting behind the counter. His eyes were closed, his head leaned against the wall, and his mouth hung slightly open. She figured he would soon start snoring. That wouldn't be good if a customer showed up.

"Are you napping?" Rachel asked, touching Grandpa's shoulder.

Grandpa's eyes popped open. "Uh, no—I was just resting my eyes."

Rachel snickered. "Mom says that sometimes when I find her on the sofa with her eyes closed."

"Like father, like daughter." Grandpa yawned and stretched his arms. "I am kind of tired this morning."

"Didn't you sleep well last night?"

He touched his left ear. "*Letscht nacht hab ich ohreweh ghat* [I had an earache last night]."

"I'm sorry to hear you had an earache. Does it feel better today?"

Grandpa nodded. "Jah, but my muscles ache from tossing and turning all night. Guess I'm just getting *alt* [old] and *schwach* [feeble]."

Rachel shook her head. "You're not so old, Grandpa, and I don't think you're feeble, either. You get around pretty well."

"Sure feels like I'm alt and schwach sometimes—especially when I have to deal with aches and pains." Grandpa pushed back his chair and stood. "I think I'll go to the house and take some aspirin. Would you keep an eye on things while I'm gone?"

"I can do that. Do you want me to do anything special while you're gone?"

"Would you water the plants?"

Rachel smiled. "I'd be glad to." Even though Rachel didn't enjoy doing chores in the house, she didn't mind working in the greenhouse at all.

"All right then; I'll be back soon," Grandpa said.

"Take your time. I can manage fine," Rachel called as Grandpa left the greenhouse.

Rachel drew in a deep breath, enjoying the fragrance of the flowers and plants growing on one side of the greenhouse. Several vases filled with cut flowers smelled equally nice.

Someday, when I'm grown up, I'd like to own a greenhouse just like this, Rachel thought as she grabbed the watering can and turned on the faucet. *I think tending flowers and plants would be a whole lot more fun than getting married and taking care of babies.*

Rachel began watering the plants closest to her. The door opened, and Audra entered the greenhouse, carrying a small paper sack.

"Hi, Rachel." Audra smiled. "I went up to the house looking for you, but your grossdaadi said you were out here."

Rachel nodded. "I'm watering plants for him while he takes aspirin for his achy muscles."

"He said I should tell you that he'll be a few

more minutes because he has to go to the phone shed to make a few calls."

Rachel shrugged. "No problem. I'm getting along fine."

"Jah, I can see." Audra held out the paper sack. "Since we couldn't go out to celebrate your birthday last night, I wanted to come by and give you your present. Hallich gebottsdaag, Rachel."

Rachel smiled as she set the watering can down and took the sack. At least someone had given her a birthday gift. She set the sack on the counter and opened it. Inside was a book about a cat named Sam, along with a gray cloth mouse.

"The book's for you," Audra said. "And I thought Cuddles would like the mouse 'cause it's filled with catnip."

"Danki," said Rachel. "I'm sure we'll both enjoy our treats."

Audra leaned on the edge of the counter. "I heard your mamm had a baby girl yesterday."

Rachel nodded. "Hannah is coming home from the hospital sometime today."

"I'll bet you're real excited."

Rachel moistened her lips. "Well, I—"

"If I had a baby sister, I'd be excited," Audra said.

Rachel motioned to the plants she'd been

watering. "Being here in the greenhouse—that's what excites me!"

"I guess it would since you like flowers so much." Audra moved toward the door. "I'd better go. My mamm needs help cleaning the house, and I told her I wouldn't be gone long."

"Okay. Danki for coming—and for the gifts." Rachel followed Audra across the room. "If we ever go for supper to celebrate my birthday, I'll let you know."

"Okay. See you later, Rachel."

Audra scurried out the door, and Rachel picked up the watering can. She'd only watered a few plants when she heard a commotion outside.

Woof! Woof!

Meow! Meow!

Woof! Woof! Woof!

Meow!

Thinking Cuddles and Buddy must be playing in the yard, Rachel set the watering can down and opened the door. "What's going on out here?" she hollered when Cuddles zipped past the greenhouse. "Why aren't you in the barn with your busslin, Cuddles?"

The cat turned and darted into the greenhouse.

Woof! Woof! Their neighbor's collie dog,

Chester, bounded in behind the cat. Well, at least it wasn't Buddy causing trouble this time.

Cuddles jumped onto the table where some new plants had been set, and Chester swatted at her tail with his paw. *Woof! Woof! Woof!*

Meow! Cuddles leaped off the table and jumped into a hanging basket full of petunias. The basket swung back and forth. Chester barked, and Cuddles laid her ears back and hissed.

Rachel knew she wouldn't be able to get Cuddles out of the petunia basket until Chester was gone, so she grabbed the collie's collar and led him toward the door.

Woof! Chester jerked free and raced to the back of the greenhouse with his tail swishing.

"Come back here, you crazy mutt!" Rachel hollered. "You'll knock something over if you're not careful!"

Rachel had no sooner said the words when— *thunk!*—Chester smacked a pot of pansies with his tail and it toppled to the floor. The pot broke and dirt went everywhere!

"Oh, no! Now look what you've done!" Rachel groaned. "You're a cute dog, but you're as rowdy as Jacob's hund!"

Rachel lunged for Chester, but he darted away.

Round and round the greenhouse they went, Chester barking, Cuddles meowing, and Rachel shouting.

Thunk! Crash! Chester knocked another pot of pansies to the floor.

"You're in big trouble now!" Rachel dashed to a faucet with a hose connected and turned on the water. She pointed the hose at Chester and shot water in his face.

Woof! Woof! Woof! Chester zipped out the open door.

Rachel slammed the door behind him and drew in a deep breath. She needed to calm down. She needed to check on Cuddles.

After turning off the water, she hurried to the hanging plants and looked up. There was no sign of her cat in the petunia basket!

"Cuddles, where are you? Come here, kitty, kitty!"

No response. Not even a faint meow.

"You can come out of hiding now, Cuddles. That mean old dog is gone. Go back to the barn and take care of your kittens. They're probably hungry." Rachel walked up and down the rows of plants, calling for Cuddles. She was about to check behind the counter when her wild-eyed cat leaped over a tray of vegetable plants sitting on the floor.

"No! No! You'll wreck the—"

Meow! Cuddles leaped into the air and—*floop!*—landed on top of a struggling cherry tomato plant, squishing it!

Rachel gasped. "If Grandpa sees the mess you and Chester made, he'll be upset. I'd better get this cleaned up before he comes back."

Just then, the door swung open. Cuddles darted outside, right between Grandpa's legs. "I'm back!" Grandpa said as he entered the building. "How's everything going?"

Before Rachel could tell Grandpa what had happened, his bushy eyebrows rose high and he pointed at the broken pots and dirt all over the floor. "What in all the world happened, Rachel?"

"I—uh—heard a commotion in the yard, and when I opened the door, Cuddles ran into the greenhouse. Then the neighbor's collie darted in after her." Rachel drew in a quick breath and pointed to the plants Chester had knocked over. "He was worse than Buddy. I had a terrible time getting him outside." She pointed to the tomato plant. "When I did get Chester out, Cuddles jumped on this and smashed it."

The wrinkles in Grandpa's forehead deepened,

and his cheek muscle quivered. "I'm very disappointed, Rachel. I thought I could depend on you to take care of things while I was gone. I didn't think I'd come back and find a mess like this!"

"I–I'm sorry. I didn't expect the dog to run in here and make a mess." She grabbed the broom leaning against the wall. "I'll clean everything up, and I'll work extra hours in the greenhouse until I've made enough money to replace the ones that were ruined."

Grandpa leaned against the workbench and folded his arms as Rachel swept up the dirt. She could almost feel him watching her. He probably thought she didn't know how to clean the mess. Did he think she couldn't do anything right?

A few minutes later, Grandpa touched Rachel's shoulder. "I'm sorry for snapping at you. This was obviously an accident. It wasn't your fault." He took the broom from her. "Let me finish sweeping while you look for your cat."

Rachel hugged him. "Danki, Grandpa."

He patted her head. "I was young once, too, you know. And I never liked being scolded for something that wasn't my fault."

Rachel smiled. She was glad she had such an understanding grandpa. She looked forward to spending more time with him in the greenhouse this summer. And she hoped no cats or dogs ever got into the greenhouse again!

Chapter 7
Hannah Comes Home

Later that afternoon, Rachel sat at the kitchen table thinking about what she might cook for supper. Her mind began to wander. She thought about Cuddles and how she wished she could keep all six of her kittens. She knew Mom would never agree, though. If she were lucky, she might be allowed to keep one kitten.

She thought about all the work she'd done and wished she could run to the creek. She'd be happy for just a few minutes—long enough to slip her feet in the water and get cooled off. It was so hot and muggy; Rachel felt she deserved a break.

Rachel was about to go to the greenhouse and ask Grandpa if she could go to the creek for a while, when she heard a horse whinny. She rushed to the window and saw Esther's horse and buggy coming up the driveway.

When Rachel stepped onto the back porch, Esther smiled and waved.

"Wie geht's?" Rachel called as she ran out to Esther's buggy.

"I'm doing well. How are things with you?"

Rachel shrugged. "Okay, I guess."

"Just okay?"

"Jah."

"You look droopy. Do you feel all right?"

"I'm not sick—just tired from working so hard."

"What have you been doing?" Esther asked.

"I fixed breakfast and lunch, did the dishes, picked up the house, and helped Grandpa in the greenhouse." Rachel sighed. "Now it's time for me to start supper. If I can think of something good to fix, that is."

"It does sound as if you've had a busy day," Esther said as she unhitched her horse from the buggy.

Rachel motioned to the house. "If you came to see Mom, she's not here. She had her boppli yesterday."

"I know about the baby. When we got back from the farmer's market our answering machine had a message saying that Mom had a baby girl named Hannah." Esther smiled. "Is Mom coming home soon?"

Rachel shrugged. "Pap went to the hospital after breakfast, but they're not here yet. You can come back later if you want."

"No need for that; I'm planning to stay. In fact, I came to make supper for the family. Rudy will join us when he's finished working." Esther reached into the buggy and pulled out a cardboard box. "I also came by to give you a birthday present."

"Oh, what is it?"

Esther set the box on the ground. "Why don't you open it and see?"

Rachel knelt down, opened the flaps on the box, and gasped when she saw what was inside. It was a shiny new skateboard, just like the one she'd put in layaway at Kauffman's store last summer!

Rachel's eyes filled with tears as she looked at Esther. "I never expected to get another skateboard—especially not one so new and nice. Danki, Esther."

"You're welcome. I knew you gave Audra your skateboard after you accidentally broke hers, so I thought you'd like to have a new one." Esther bent and hugged Rachel. "I'm sorry for not getting the gift to you on time, but I want to wish you a happy birthday now, little sister."

"It's okay," Rachel said. "With Hannah being

born on my birthday, I think everyone in the family forgot about me. I wish Hannah had been born on a different day."

"Women don't get to choose the day or time their babies will be born," Esther said. "I'm sure you were disappointed that you didn't get to have supper out, but I don't want you to think everyone forgot about you."

"I know you didn't, or else you wouldn't have given me the skateboard."

"That's right, and I'm sure Mom and Pap will give you something besides a baby sister when she gets home from the hospital and is settled in." Esther reached into the buggy again and pulled out a paper sack. "In the meantime, I brought everything we'll need for supper. So if you can carry this sack and your skateboard, would you take it to the house while I put my horse away?"

Rachel nodded. "I can manage both. When you come inside, I'll help you make supper."

"Wouldn't you like to try your new skateboard?"

"Maybe later. The only good place I have to skateboard is in the barn, and it's too stuffy in there right now." Rachel blew out her breath so hard the ties on her *kapp* [cap] floated up. "With all this hot weather, I feel like a wet noodle."

Esther chuckled. "Then why don't you go to the creek and cool off?"

"What about supper?"

"I can manage on my own." Esther squeezed Rachel's shoulder. "I'll ring the dinner bell when I need you to come and set the table. How's that sound?"

"It sounds real good. Danki." Rachel smiled at Esther. "See you later then."

Rachel took the sack of groceries to the kitchen and rushed to the barn to put away her new skateboard.

"Where are you going, pretty bird?" she sang as she sprinted for the creek. "Where are you going, pretty bird? I am going to my tree, I am going to my tree, I am going to my tree, sweet Rose."

After getting such a nice birthday gift from Esther, Rachel felt better about life. When Esther had suggested she go to the creek, she felt loved and appreciated. Maybe things weren't as bad as she thought. Maybe when Pap brought Mom and the baby home from the hospital, they would have a birthday present for her to open.

Rachel sat on a big rock by the creek. She dangled her bare feet in the cool water and wiggled her toes. After working so hard all day, she was glad to sit and relax. She felt even better to know she didn't have to fix supper this evening.

She leaned her head back and watched puffy clouds float lazily across the sky. It was so peaceful and quiet by the creek. The only sound was the steady gurgling of the water rolling over the rocks. Her eyes felt heavy, and she let them close. If she sat here long, she could easily fall asleep.

"Yahoo! This will sure feel good!"

Rachel's eyes snapped open to see Jacob barrel into the creek. Sloshing through the water, he kicked and splashed, sending water all over Rachel's dress.

"Cut that out!" she shouted. "You're getting me all wet!"

"If you don't want to be wet then you shouldn't be here at the creek!" Jacob splashed more water in her direction and laughed.

Rachel jumped up and, using her foot, splashed him right back. "How do you like that, Jacob Yoder?"

"I like it just fine. The cool water feels good on a hot day like this!" Jacob played in the creek, laughing and making ripples of water go in all directions. Then he dropped to his knees, leaned over, and dunked his head under the water.

When he came up he shook his head like a dog, showering Rachel with even more water. She had to admit it felt pretty good, and it gave her some relief from the sticky summer day.

"Maybe we should go to the house and put on our swimsuits," she said. "Then we can get as wet as we like."

"Good idea. Last one to the house has to feed Buddy his supper tonight!"

"No way!" Rachel shook her head. "I'm not feeding your mutt ever again, so I won't race you to the house after all!"

Jacob shrugged. "Suit yourself." He dashed away, and Rachel sprinted behind him. She was halfway there when—*ding! ding! ding!*—the dinner bell rang.

"That must be Esther," Rachel said. "She's at the house fixing supper and said she'd ring the bell when she needed me to set the table."

"Does that mean you're not going swimming?" Jacob asked.

"Probably not, and if supper's almost ready, you won't be going swimming, either." Rachel hurried past Jacob and ran to the house. "Ha! Ha! I won the race!" she shouted as Jacob stomped up the steps behind her.

"So what? It doesn't matter who won the race, because I was planning to feed Buddy anyway!"

When Rachel entered the kitchen she encountered a wonderful aroma. "Mmm. . .what are you cooking?" she asked, stepping to the stove where Esther stirred something in a large kettle.

Esther smiled at Rachel. "Chicken and dumplings. There's also a tossed green salad and some pickled beets in the refrigerator."

Rachel licked her lips. She knew Jacob liked chicken and dumplings, and she loved pickled beets, so they would both enjoy this meal!

"Do you need me to do anything besides setting the table?" she asked Esther.

"You can peel some carrots when you're done if you like."

"Okay."

Rachel had just finished setting the table when she heard a vehicle rumble into the yard. She rushed to the window to see Pap help Mom out of Harold's van. Mom held the baby in her arms.

Esther opened the back door and rushed outside. Rachel was right behind her.

"Welcome home!" Esther said when Mom and Pap stepped onto the porch. "I got your message about the boppli. How are you feeling, Mom?"

"I'm pretty tired but doing okay." Mom glanced at Rachel. "How are things here at the house? Did you manage okay while I was gone?"

"Things are fine," Rachel said. "Esther came over to fix supper, and I just set the table."

Pap smiled at Mom. "Aren't we fortunate to have two thoughtful *dechder* [daughters]?"

Mom nodded.

"Speaking of your daughters," Esther said, pointing to herself, "your oldest daughter is eager to hold her new baby sister."

"Why don't we all go into the living room?" Pap suggested. "Then you can get to know our sweet little Hannah."

Esther smiled. "That suits me just fine!"

Rachel followed Mom, Esther, and Pap into the living room. Esther sat in the rocking chair, and Mom placed the baby in Esther's lap. Then she sat on the sofa, and Rachel sat beside her.

Pap moved toward the door. "I think I'll walk to the fields and let the boys know we're home. I'd also like to see how they've managed in my absence." He turned around and looked at Rachel. "Where's your grossdaadi?"

"Grandpa's still at the greenhouse," Rachel replied. "I'm sure he'll be coming in soon for supper, though."

"I expect you're right about that." Pap bent over and gave the baby a peck on the cheek; then he hurried out the door.

As Esther rocked the baby with a dreamy look on her face, she sang a lullaby. Then she looked at Mom and smiled. "You are so blessed to have such a sweet little boppli."

Mom nodded as tears welled in her eyes. "You'll feel the same blessing in a few months, after your boppli is born."

"Jah, I'm sure I will." Esther looked at Rachel. "There's a gift for the boppli in the paper sack I brought with the supper items. It's sitting on the kitchen counter. Would you get it for me?"

"Okay." As Rachel walked past the rocking chair, she glanced at her baby sister. Hannah's eyes were closed, and her little chest rose up and down as she breathed. She looked so peaceful nestled in Esther's arms. Rachel wondered if she had been that tiny and cute when she was a baby. If so, no one had ever mentioned it to her. Eleven whole years had passed since she'd been born; maybe they'd forgotten what she had been like when she was that little.

"Oh, Rachel, one more thing," Esther called.

"What's that?"

"While you're in the kitchen, would you check on the chicken and dumplings?"

"Sure, no problem."

When Rachel entered the kitchen, she lifted the lid on the kettle and sniffed. "Yum. . .this sure smells good." Her stomach rumbled. "I can hardly wait until supper!"

Rachel found the gift and took it to the living room. "Here you go," she said, handing it to Mom.

Mom tore the wrapping off and removed a pair of pink baby booties and a matching cap. "These are so nice. Did you knit them, Esther?"

Esther nodded. "I made a blue set, too. . .in case you had a *buwe* [boy]."

"Maybe you'll have a buwe," Mom said. "Then he can wear the other set."

Esther sighed and nestled Hannah against her shoulder. "I think Rudy wants a buwe, and I hope he won't be disappointed if it's a *maedel* [girl]."

"Why would he be disappointed if you had a girl?" Rachel questioned.

"I think he'd like a boy to carry on his name and to help him on the farm," Esther said.

Rachel folded her arms. "Well, I hope you have a maedel. We don't need any more buwe in this family."

Mom clicked her tongue. "We shall all love your boppli whether it's a buwe or a maedel."

Esther kissed the top of Hannah's head. "That's right, and we'll love this little one, too, because she's a real sweetie."

Mom nodded. "I feel so blessed to have a new baby daughter. I'm pleased that our two little ones will only be a few months apart." She smiled at Esther. "They can grow up together, and hopefully they'll become good friends."

"That's what I hope for, too," Esther said.

A pang of jealousy stabbed Rachel's heart. Did Mom and Esther care more about Hannah and Esther's baby than about her? When Esther's baby was born, would Rachel be ignored even more than she was now?

"I guess I'll go cut up those carrots now," Rachel mumbled as she shuffled toward the kitchen.

Esther started singing to the baby again.

Tears rolled down Rachel's cheeks as she entered the kitchen. She felt so forgotten. Mom hadn't even told her happy birthday last night or today, either. Mom and Esther could only talk about babies! Rachel probably wouldn't get a birthday present from Mom and Pap this year at all!

If I ever do get married and have any bopplin, Rachel thought, *I'll make sure their birthdays are always special! I'll make sure they get a nice gift every year, too.*

Chapter 8

Nothing but Trouble

Wa-a-a! Wa-a-a! Wa-a-a!

Rachel covered her ears with her pillow and moaned. Her baby sister might be cute and cuddly, but she sure did cry a lot. In the three weeks since Mom had brought Hannah home from the hospital, every night Rachel was awakened by the baby's cries. How was she supposed to do her chores when she couldn't get a good night's sleep?

She wondered if Hannah's crying bothered anyone else. If so, they hadn't said anything. In fact, the only thing Mom and Pap said about Hannah was how cute she was, and how blessed they felt to have a baby in the house again. Even Grandpa, Henry, and Jacob made over Hannah with silly baby sounds.

Wa-a-a! Wa-a-a! The irritating cries from Mom and Pap's bedroom continued to float up the stairs.

Rachel pushed the pillow tighter against her ears, hoping to drown out the sound. It was no use. Hannah's cries seemed to be getting louder.

With an exasperated sigh, Rachel pulled her sheet aside and crawled out of bed. She plodded over to the window and lifted the shade, squinting at the rising sun.

I guess if the sun's up, I may as well be, too, she decided. *Audra's birthday is just a few weeks away. Maybe I can paint a rock for her before I help Mom with breakfast.*

Rachel frowned. They still hadn't gone out for her birthday supper, and she'd almost given up on the idea. She'd asked Pap several times, but he always said they would do it later—as soon as Mom felt stronger, and when he and the brothers weren't so busy.

Maybe Mom would never feel up to going out for supper. Maybe she'd be tired for a long time, the way their neighbor, Anna Miller, was after her last baby was born.

Pushing her troubling thoughts aside, Rachel gathered up her painting supplies, picked out a nicely shaped rock, and headed downstairs. She'd just set everything on the kitchen table when Mom stepped into the room.

"*Guder mariye* [Good morning], Rachel," Mom said. "I'm surprised to see you up so early."

Rachel yawned. "I couldn't sleep. The baby woke me with all that crying."

"She was hungry." Mom smiled. "She's been fed and had her windel changed, so she's sleeping peacefully again."

"That figures," Rachel mumbled.

"What?"

"Oh, nothing."

Mom motioned to the table. "I'm going to start breakfast, so you'll need to put your paints away and set the table."

Rachel frowned. "Since it's so early, I figured I'd have plenty of time to paint a rock for Audra's birthday before you started breakfast."

"I thought you planned to give Audra one of Cuddles's kittens."

"I do, but I want to give her a painted animal rock before she and her family leave for Sarasota, Florida."

"Oh, I didn't realize they were going to Florida," Mom said.

Rachel nodded. "Her grandparents live there, and they invited Audra's family to celebrate Audra's birthday with them."

"Oh, I see."

Rachel motioned to the rock sitting on the table. "Since the kittens aren't quite old enough to leave their mamm, I wanted to give Audra something for her birthday before she leaves."

"That makes sense," Mom said with a nod, "but you'll have to paint some other time. Your daed wants to get an early start in the fields this morning, before it becomes too hot. So we'll need to eat an early breakfast."

Rachel sighed. "Okay, Mom."

"Speaking of birthdays," Mom said, "I've been meaning to give you the gift your daed picked up for your birthday when he was in town the other day. We're late with your gift this year because of Hannah being born on your birthday."

Anticipation welled in Rachel's chest. "Where is it?" she asked excitedly.

Mom pointed to the cupboard where she kept her sewing supplies. "It's in there."

Rachel stared at the cupboard. She hoped it wasn't another sewing kit like the one Mom had given her last year. Rachel didn't like to sew much, and she certainly didn't need two sewing kits!

"Go ahead and get it," Mom said. "It's in a cardboard box on the bottom shelf."

Rachel opened the cupboard door and took out the box. She set it on the table and opened the lid. A blue-eyed, blond-haired baby doll, dressed in Amish clothes, stared back at her. Rachel took it out of the box and faced Mom. "You bought me a baby doll for my birthday?"

Mom smiled. "Actually, your daed got the doll, but that's what I told him to get."

"Why? I already have the faceless doll Audra gave me, and you know I hardly ever play with it."

Mom's cheeks turned pink. "Well, I—I thought, with you having a baby sister now, you might like to play with the doll and pretend to feed it whenever I'm feeding Hannah."

Rachel swallowed around the lump in her throat. *It figures that my gift would have something to do with Hannah.* "Maybe I'll set the doll on my dresser," she said. "Then when Hannah's old enough, I'll let her play with it."

Wrinkles formed in Mom's forehead. "Don't you like the doll?"

Rachel bit her lower lip as she tried to think of something to say that wouldn't be a lie or hurt Mom's feelings. "The doll's nice," she said, "but I'm getting too big to play with dolls. So if you don't mind, I'll just set it on my dresser."

Mom shook her head. "I don't mind, but—"

"I'll put these paints away now." Rachel scooped up the bottles of paint, put them in the box, and forced a smile. "Danki for the birthday present, Mom."

Before Mom could reply, Rachel scurried out the back door and set the box of paints on the little table on the porch. She was afraid if she stayed in the kitchen one minute longer she would burst into tears. Mom still saw her as a little girl who played with dolls. Mom was so busy with the baby she couldn't even see that Rachel was growing up and might want something more exciting for her birthday than a baby doll.

"I guess things will never be the same around here now that Hannah's living with us," Rachel mumbled. "I guess no one will think much about me ever again."

Rachel had just finished drying the breakfast dishes when Mom said, "I'm going to the cellar to wash some clothes. When I'm done, I'd like you to hang them on the line while I feed the boppli."

Rachel sighed. More work. Maybe she could get out her paints while Mom washed clothes. She could probably finish painting the rock before it was time to hang the laundry on the line.

"One more thing," Mom said as she started for the door.

"What's that?" Rachel asked.

"While I'm washing the clothes, I'd like you to watch Hannah."

Rachel frowned. "I thought she was sleeping."

Mom nodded. "She is—in her cradle in the living room. Of course she might not stay asleep."

"What should I do if she wakes up and starts crying?"

"Give her the pacifier."

"Oh, okay."

Mom left the kitchen, and Rachel picked up another dish to dry. She figured if Hannah woke up while she was painting, it wouldn't take much time to put the pacifier in her mouth. Then she could get right back to work on the rock.

Rachel soon had all her paints laid out on the table. She picked up her brush, dipped it into the black paint, and was getting ready to paint the body of the ladybug, when—*Wa-a-a! Wa-a-a!*—the baby's shrill cry almost caused her to jump out of her seat.

"Oh, great!" Rachel set the rock aside and

hurried into the living room. The pacifier wasn't in the cradle with Hannah, and she didn't see it on the table by the sofa, either. Maybe Mom had left it in the bedroom.

Rachel ran into her parents' room and looked around. She didn't see the pacifier anywhere.

Wa-a-a! Wa-a-a! Wa-a-a! Baby Hannah's cries grew louder.

Rachel dashed from the room and down the cellar stairs. She found Mom bent over their gas-operated washing machine with a pair of trousers in her hand.

"What are you doing down here, Rachel?" Mom asked. "Can't you hear the boppli crying?"

"I hear her all right." Rachel frowned. "I can't make her stop crying because the pacifier's gone."

"I'm sure it's in her cradle."

"I didn't see it."

Mom's glasses had slipped to the end of her nose, and she pushed them back in place. "You'd better look again."

"Okay." Rachel tromped back up the stairs. At this rate she would never get Audra's ladybug rock painted!

When Rachel entered the living room, the baby's cries grew louder, and her little face had turned bright red.

Rachel covered her ears. She wished Mom wasn't washing clothes. She wished the baby would stop crying. She wished she could find that pacifier!

Wa-a-a! Wa-a-a! Hannah's face turned redder.

Rachel put her fingers to her lips. "Shh. . . . Please go back to sleep."

Hannah continued to wail.

Maybe a song will help, Rachel thought. She leaned close to the cradle and began to sing. "*Bisht du an schlaufa; bish du an schlaufa? Schweschder Hannah, Schweschder Hanna? Ich hei-ah die bells an ringa. Ich hei-ah die bells an ringa.* [Are you sleeping; are you sleeping? Sister Hannah, Sister Hannah? Morning bells are ringing. Morning bells are ringing.] Ding-dong-ding! Ding-dong-ding!"

Hannah stopped crying for a few seconds, then she scrunched up her nose and let loose with a shrill—*Wa-a-a-a-a!*

Rachel rocked the cradle back and forth. Hannah cried. Rachel made silly faces. Hannah cried more.

In desperation, Rachel reached into the cradle and picked up Hannah. To her surprise, there was the pacifier—right where the baby had been lying!

Rachel placed Hannah back in the cradle and

put the pacifier in her mouth.

Hannah's lips moved in and out as she sucked on the pacifier. Rachel sighed with relief.

She hurried back to the kitchen, dipped her brush into the paint, and had finished half of the ladybug's body when—*Wa-a-a! Wa-a-a!*—Hannah began to wail.

Rachel groaned. "No! No! Not again! Is there no end to my troubles?"

She set the rock down and returned to the living room. Hannah's face had turned red again, and she waved her little hands. The pacifier had fallen out of her mouth; this time it was beside her.

Rachel put the pacifier in Hannah's mouth; then she headed back to the kitchen. She'd just sat down when the baby started howling again.

"I give up!" Rachel marched to the living room, picked up the baby, and sat in the rocking chair. She remembered how Hannah had fallen asleep when Esther had rocked her. She hoped that might work now.

Squeak. . .squeak. . .squeak. The old chair protested as she rocked back and forth. Soon Hannah's cries turned to soft snores, and Rachel knew Hannah had finally fallen asleep.

She was getting ready to put the baby back

in her cradle when Mom stepped into the room. "I'm glad to see you holding the boppli," she said, smiling at Rachel. "You haven't held her much since we brought her home."

"She kept crying, and nothing helped. So I decided to try rocking her." Rachel nodded at the cradle. "I was just getting ready to put her back to bed."

"The clothes are washed and the basket's sitting by the clothesline," Mom said, taking the baby from Rachel. "I feel tired, so I think I'll rest a bit while you hang the clothes out to dry."

"Okay. When that's done I'm going back to the kitchen to finish painting Audra's ladybug rock."

Mom shook her head. "You'll have to find another place to do that, Rachel. After I catch my breath, I need to cut out some material to make a few dresses for Hannah. I need the table for that."

Rachel fought the urge to bite her fingernail. Everything seemed to revolve around her baby sister these days, and nobody cared about her.

As she started across the room, Mom called, "Why don't you take your paints outside? After you hang the laundry you can use the little table on the porch to paint Audra's rock."

"I guess I could do that." Rachel went to the

kitchen, gathered her painting supplies, and carried them to the porch. Then she dashed across the yard, reached into the basket for a towel, and hung it on the line.

As she took out another towel, she spotted Jacob's dog lying on the porch with his nose tucked between his paws. She figured Buddy was asleep, but just in case, she would hurry to get the towels hung on the line. The last thing she needed was for him to grab a towel and tear it to shreds, as he'd done one other time.

When the towels were all hung, Rachel stepped onto the porch and opened a jar of black paint. At last, she could paint Audra's rock.

"What are you up to?" Grandpa asked when he stepped out the back door.

"I'm painting a ladybug rock for Audra," Rachel said. "Her birthday's coming, and I want her to have it before she leaves for Florida."

"I'll bet it'll be hot in Florida this time of the year," Grandpa said as he sat on the porch swing.

Rachel dabbed her sweaty forehead with the corner of her apron. "It's hot here, too."

He nodded. "Jah, hot and plenty humid."

"Why aren't you working in your greenhouse?" Rachel asked.

"I haven't had much business this morning so

I decided to close it and come to the house for a nap."

"Didn't you sleep well last night?"

He shook his head. "Hannah's crying kept me awake, and since she's crying right now, I decided to see if I could catch a few winks on the porch."

"Well, don't let me stop you," Rachel said. "I'll quietly paint Audra's rock, and I promise not to make any noise."

"I appreciate that." Grandpa leaned his head against the back of the swing and closed his eyes. Soon he began to snore softly.

Buddy got up and plodded across the porch. He stood by the swing and nudged Grandpa's hand with his nose. Grandpa didn't budge. Rachel figured he must be really tired.

Grandpa's snores grew louder. Buddy tilted his head and whined.

"Be quiet, Buddy," Rachel said. "If you wake Grandpa, I'll put you back in your dog run where you belong."

Buddy plodded over to Rachel, and—*slurp! slurp!*—licked her face.

"Stop that, you hairy mutt!" Rachel pushed the dog aside and dipped her brush into the paint.

Oomph! Buddy bumped into the table, knocking

the jar of paint over and spilling some onto the porch.

"Now look what you've done!" Rachel shook her finger at Buddy. "You're nothing but trouble!"

She dashed into the yard and grabbed the hose. Then she squirted the paint with water.

Woof! Woof! Buddy bumped Rachel's hand with his big nose. Water shot out of the hose and hit Grandpa right in the face!

"Yeow!" Grandpa jumped off the swing. "What are you doing, child?" He pointed his finger at Rachel. "Why'd you squirt me with the hose?"

"I–I'm sorry, Grandpa. I—I didn't do it on purpose." Rachel ran into the yard, turned off the hose, and stepped onto the porch. "I was trying to wash off the paint Buddy made me spill on the porch, and then the mangy critter bumped my arm and the hose got you."

Grandpa wiped his face with his shirtsleeve and motioned to the greenhouse. "Looks like I've got a customer, so I guess it's a good thing I woke up. I just didn't expect such a cold awakening." He started down the steps but turned back around. "You'd better put Buddy in his dog run. I don't want him coming out to the greenhouse and bothering my customer."

"I'll see to it right away."

Grandpa was halfway across the yard when Rachel called, "Do you need my help in the greenhouse?"

He shook his head. "No thanks. I can manage this afternoon."

Disappointed, Rachel reached for Buddy's collar, but he dashed across the porch, slid into one of Mom's flower pots, and darted into the yard.

Rachel ran after him, waving her hands. "Come back here, you troublesome dog!"

Woof! Woof! Woof! Buddy ran in circles, then took off toward the barn.

Rachel dashed after him, slipped on a pile of hay inside the barn, and landed on her knees. "Trouble. . .trouble. . .trouble," she mumbled. "I'm so sick of all this trouble!"

Buddy screeched to a halt, pranced up to Rachel, and—*slurp!*—licked her nose.

She grabbed his collar. "You're coming with me, you hairy, bad-breathed brute."

Slurp! Slurp! The dog gave Rachel's nose a couple more swipes with his big wet tongue.

Holding tightly to Buddy's collar, Rachel led him across the yard. When they reached his dog run, she opened the gate and ushered him in.

"You're nothing but trouble," she muttered as she slammed the gate. "But at least you won't cause me any more trouble today!"

Chapter 9
A Thrilling Ride

A trickle of sweat rolled down Rachel's forehead and nearly ran into her eyes. With the corner of her apron, she wiped it from her forehead. Pap, Henry, and Jacob were in the fields this morning; Grandpa was working in his greenhouse; and Mom had taken the baby to the doctor's for a checkup. Rachel had been left at home to clean her room. She'd already made her bed, swept the floor, and washed the windows. Now she sat on the floor going through some old things she'd found in her dresser drawer.

"I wish I didn't have so many chores to do. It's not fair that I never get to do anything fun. I wish I could help Grandpa in the greenhouse today," Rachel grumbled as she tossed two broken pencils into the trash can.

Tears stung her eyes, and she removed her

glasses to wipe her face. When she put the glasses back on she noticed a smudge on the lens. "Oh, great, now I can barely see!" She took her glasses off and placed them on the dresser, then went to the window and looked out. Everything in the yard looked blurry without her glasses, reminding Rachel that she needed to wear them all the time.

When she'd first gotten the glasses, she hadn't liked them at all—especially when boys at school had called her "four eyes." Eventually the boys quit their teasing, and Rachel had gotten used to wearing her glasses. She'd also realized that wearing glasses didn't make her look ugly or stupid. In fact, Audra said glasses made Rachel look smart.

Rachel put the glasses back on and continued to stare out the window. Even with the smudge she could see Cuddles and her little ones frolicking in the grass. The kittens were getting so big. By the time Audra and her family got back from Sarasota, the kittens should be old enough to leave their mother. Then she could give Audra the one she'd picked out.

Rachel thought about how excited Audra had been when she'd given her the ladybug rock the night before. She'd told Rachel that she and her family would leave on the bus for Sarasota this morning. She said she'd take the painted rock as a reminder that she had a friend waiting to greet her when she returned home.

"At least someone still likes me," Rachel mumbled as she moved away from the window and sat on the floor. "I used to feel like part of the family until Hannah came. Now, unless someone needs me for something, I'm ignored. I bet they love Hannah more than they do me. I bet they wouldn't even know if I was gone."

Tears streamed down Rachel's face, and her nose started to run. "I'm only good for work, work, work. I should run away from home!" She choked on a sob. "If I went away and never came back, that would show them!" *Sniff! Sniff!* "But where would I go? If I went over to Grandma Yoder's or Aunt Karen's, they'd send me right home. I can't go to Audra's house because she's in Florida."

She turned away from the window. "Orlie's folks wouldn't let me stay there, either, but I could walk over to Orlie's and show him my new skateboard. I shouldn't have to stay in this hot, stuffy house and do nothing but work!"

Rachel put the drawer back in the dresser, slipped on her sneakers, put on her kapp, and hurried from the room.

When she got downstairs, she cleaned her glasses at the kitchen sink and dried them with a clean dishtowel. She figured she would be back from Orlie's before Mom got home, but just in case, she wrote a note saying where she'd gone and left it on the table. Then she went to the barn, got her skateboard, and headed toward Orlie's house.

As Rachel walked along, she was tempted to ride her skateboard, but then she remembered that Mom had warned her not to ride it near the road. So, she carried the skateboard under one arm and walked in the tall grass near the shoulder of the road.

As Rachel trudged along, she thought about last summer, and how she and her family had gone on a picnic the day school let out. They'd had so much fun—until she'd fallen into the pond and had gotten her clothes wet and muddy. They'd also had several barbecues last summer, eaten a few meals at restaurants, played in the creek, gone to the farmer's market, and made several batches of delicious homemade ice cream.

This summer it seemed that Rachel had done nothing but work. Even being in Grandpa's greenhouse involved work, although she did enjoy that more than any other work. Rachel wondered if she would have any real fun before it was time to return to school.

She kicked a stone with her sneaker and grunted. It would be hard to go back to school and listen to the other scholars tell about the family trips and the other fun things they'd done. All Rachel would have to talk about was her new baby sister, and how she was expected to do more work now that Hannah lived with them.

Beep! Beep!

Rachel whirled around as a blue convertible pulled onto the shoulder of the road. She recognized the blond-haired English girl in the passenger's seat. It was Sherry. A teenage boy sat in the driver's seat, but Rachel had never met him.

"Hi, Rachel," Sherry called. "Where are you going with that neat-looking skateboard?"

"I'm heading to my friend Orlie's house to show him what my sister gave me for my birthday," Rachel replied.

"It looks nice," Sherry said. "Have you tried it out yet?"

Rachel shook her head. "Where are you going? Are you headed to the farmer's market?"

"Nope. We're on our way to Hershey Park," the boy said.

Rachel felt envious. "I've always wanted to visit Hershey Park," she said, staring at the ground.

"Would your folks let you go with us?" Sherry asked. "We could drive you home so you could ask."

Rachel looked up. *Thump! Thump! Thump!* Her heart hammered in her chest like a woodpecker tapping on the trunk of a tree. She would really like to spend the day at Hershey Park, and she'd give almost anything to take a ride in a convertible.

She moistened her lips with her tongue as she thought. "My mom's not at home right now, and my dad and brothers are in the fields, so there's really no one to ask."

Rachel thought about Grandpa. She knew he was working in his greenhouse. She also knew she should ask him before she went anywhere with Sherry and Dave. But since she'd left a note on the table saying she was going to Orlie's, she didn't think her family would worry if they came into the house and found her gone. Besides, she probably wouldn't even be missed—unless someone wanted a chore done.

Rachel smiled at Sherry. "I'd be happy to go to Hershey Park with you."

"Great!" Sherry motioned to the teenage boy beside her. "This is my brother, Dave. He's almost eighteen, and he's a really good driver."

Rachel smiled. "It's nice to meet you."

"Same here." Dave pointed to the back seat. "Climb in, and buckle up. Then we'll be on our way!"

Rachel climbed in, put her skateboard on the floor, buckled her seatbelt, and removed her glasses so they wouldn't fall off during the ride, which she was sure would be fast and exciting. She could hardly believe the very thing she'd dreamed about for such a long time was coming true. Not only was she going to Hershey Park, but she was about to take a ride in a shiny blue convertible!

Dave pulled the car onto the road and turned on the radio.

Rachel gasped as a gust of wind hit her in the face. It seemed like they were going awfully fast— much faster than their horse and buggy could go! Much faster than she imagined a convertible would go, either.

The ties on Rachel's kapp whipped around her face, and suddenly—*whoosh!*—the kapp lifted right off her head and sailed away with the wind. "Stop! My kapp blew off!" Rachel shouted.

Dave kept driving. Between the noise of the wind and the blaring radio, she knew he probably hadn't heard what she'd said.

Rachel tapped him on the shoulder.

"What do you want?"

"My kapp blew off. We need to stop so I can get it!"

Dave shook his head. "There's no way I'm stopping for your kapp. Besides, some car's probably run over it by now."

Rachel swallowed hard. When she returned home without her kapp, how would she explain things to Mom? She knew she'd be in trouble if she said she'd taken a ride in Dave's car without anyone's permission, but she also knew it was wrong to lie. If she got home before Mom, maybe she wouldn't have to say anything about where she'd been. But what reason would she give for not wearing her kapp?

I'll deal with it later, Rachel decided.

"I'm sorry about your kapp," Sherry called over her shoulder. "Do you have another one at home?"

"I do, but—" Rachel's voice was drowned out when Dave turned the radio up. She leaned back in her seat, realizing she could do nothing about her kapp. *I may as well relax and enjoy the ride,* she decided.

As they approached the freeway, the car sped up. Rachel thought it was exciting to go so fast, but it was also frightening. She wasn't used to traveling this fast. And that loud music put her nerves on edge. It was worse than Hannah's crying!

By the time they pulled into the parking lot at Hershey Park, Rachel felt so jittery she couldn't catch her breath. She slipped her glasses on and looked around. Cars and people were everywhere!

"We'll ride the tram to the park," Dave said. "It'll be quicker than walking."

Rachel's heart beat faster as they sat near the back of the tram. She had finally ridden in a convertible, and soon she'd go on some exciting rides inside Hershey Park. What a fun day this was turning out to be!

The man driving the tram explained that Hershey Park opened in 1907 as a place for the employees of the Hershey Chocolate Factory to picnic and have fun. He said it offered sixty attractions, including ten different roller coasters.

As they approached the park, their driver pointed to a large building. "That's Hershey's Chocolate World," he said. "You can take a free ride inside the building that will show you how candy is made, and you'll learn a lot of interesting information about the cocoa beans harvested in the jungles of Brazil."

Dave grinned at Rachel. "If we have time we

might take a tour of Chocolate World, but I think we'll probably stay busy going on all the rides inside Hershey Park. Besides, we can buy candy at the concession stands in the park."

The mention of candy made Rachel's mouth water.

When the tram stopped in front of the main gate, Rachel, Sherry, and Dave stepped out. "Now we need to purchase tickets." Dave looked at Rachel. "I hope you brought plenty of money along, because there's lots of good food in the park, not to mention all the souvenirs."

Rachel's mouth felt so dry she could barely swallow. She hadn't even thought about needing money. Tears welled in her eyes. It didn't look like she'd visit Hershey Park after all. It looked like she'd stay right here while Dave and Sherry had all the fun.

Chapter 10

An Exciting Day

"What's wrong? You look like you're gonna cry." Sherry touched Rachel's arm. "I thought you'd be happy to be at Hershey Park."

"I—I didn't bring my purse, so I have no money." Rachel choked back tears. "I guess I won't be able to see Hershey Park after all."

"It's okay," Sherry said. "Dave has plenty of money. I'm sure he'll pay for all of us."

"Oh, no, that wouldn't be right. I couldn't accept—"

"It's no big deal," Dave said. "I'll be glad to pay your way in." He winked at Rachel. "And when you get hungry, I'll even buy you some lunch."

Rachel smiled. "Thank you."

"You're welcome."

When they entered the park, Rachel couldn't believe her eyes. She'd never seen so many people in one place—not even at the farmer's market!

Rachel's stomach rumbled as they passed a stand selling hot dogs, and her mouth watered when she spotted a young girl eating pink cotton candy. Her nose twitched as they approached stands selling hamburgers, French fries, peanuts, and popcorn. All the delicious smells made her feel hungry.

As they walked on, colorful balloons caught Rachel's attention. Then she saw stuffed animals in all sizes, wild looking hats, and shiny trinkets being given as prizes for games won on the midway.

"Never mind those things," Dave said, leading the way toward the rides. "We've got more important things to do."

Rachel heard laughter and shrill screams coming from the whirly-looking ride ahead. Being at Hershey Park was better than anything she could have imagined!

"Let's go on some rides before we eat." Sherry tugged on Rachel's arm. "If we eat first we might get sick when we ride all those wild roller coasters."

Wild roller coasters? Rachel's stomach flip-flopped. If riding a roller coaster might make her sick, she wasn't sure she wanted to ride one.

"Maybe we should go on that!" Rachel pointed

to a ride called the Lady Bug.

"No way!" Sherry wrinkled her nose. "That's a baby ride, Rachel."

"How about the Bizzy Bees or Frog Hopper?" Rachel pointed to one ride, and then the other.

"You've got to be kidding!" Dave snorted. "We didn't come here to go on kiddy rides!"

Rachel motioned to the carousel. "Can we go on that?"

"I guess so," Sherry said with a nod. "I always enjoy riding the carousel."

"Not me!" Dave shook his head. "I'm getting in line for the Sooper Dooper Looper roller coaster ride!"

"You go ahead," Sherry said. "Rachel and I will ride the carousel, and then we might ride on the Dry Gulch Railroad. After that we'll meet you in front of the Ferris wheel."

Dave shrugged. "Sounds good to me. See you soon."

Rachel's excitement mounted as she stepped onto the carousel. She climbed on a shiny black horse and took the reins in her hands.

Sherry climbed onto a brown and white horse beside Rachel.

The music started, and the carousel went round

and round—slowly at first—then faster. Rachel giggled as her horse moved up and down in time to the music. "This is so much fun!" she shouted.

Sherry nodded. "Just wait until we go on the Ferris wheel!"

Rachel couldn't imagine that the Ferris wheel could be any better than this, but she was eager to try it.

When the carousel ride was over, the girls rode the train, modeled after an old steam-powered railroad. Rachel had never been on a train before, but she knew some Amish people who had ridden across the country by train.

"Are you still having fun?" Sherry asked when they stepped off the train.

Rachel nodded. "Oh yes! This is exciting!"

"I hope you don't get in trouble when you get home," Sherry said.

Rachel gulped. She wished Sherry hadn't brought that up. *If Mom gets home before I do and reads my note, she'll think I went to Orlie's house. Maybe I won't have to tell her I went to Hershey Park.*

Sherry nudged Rachel's arm. "Did you hear what I said?"

Rachel nodded. "I'm having too much fun to worry about what will happen when I get home. I don't want anything to ruin this exciting day."

"All right then, let's get over to the Ferris wheel and meet Dave!"

Rachel followed Sherry. Her excitement mounted with each step. She wondered if riding the Ferris wheel would be anything like swinging on one of the swings in the schoolyard.

Dave was there waiting when Rachel and Sherry arrived at the Ferris wheel. "How was the roller coaster?" Sherry asked.

Dave grinned, and his eyes sparkled. "It was awesome!"

"We had fun on the carousel and train ride," Rachel said.

Dave grunted. "I can only imagine."

Sherry tugged her brother's shirtsleeve. "Are you ready to go on the Ferris wheel?"

Dave shook his head. "You two go ahead. I'll stay here and watch."

"Are you afraid of heights?" Rachel asked.

"Of course not. I just rode the Sooper Dooper Looper, and that's taller than the Ferris wheel."

"Then why don't you want to ride with us?"

"Because the Ferris wheel is boring."

"No, it's not!" Sherry grabbed Rachel's hand. "Come on, Rachel. We don't need him to have fun."

As Rachel and Sherry sat down, the man running the Ferris wheel said, "Have you been on this ride before?"

Sherry nodded, but Rachel shook her head. "This is my first time at Hershey Park."

"Then you're in for a treat!" He snapped the bar across their laps. "This Ferris wheel goes nearly a hundred feet in the air, and it's sure to give you a thrill."

Rachel had never been afraid of heights until she'd fallen from a tree and broken her arm. So she was a little nervous about riding the Ferris wheel, but she wouldn't tell Sherry that, because she was also sure it would be fun.

As each car in the Ferris wheel filled with people, Rachel and Sherry's car went higher and higher. Finally, they were at the very top.

When Rachel looked down, she felt dizzy. The people below looked like ants. This was a lot higher than being in a tree or in the hayloft.

The Ferris wheel turned around and around, bringing them close the ground, then back up again. "This is so much fun!" Sherry shouted. "What an exciting day!"

Rachel nodded. "If I never get to visit another amusement park, I'll remember this day for the rest of my life!"

When the Ferris wheel stopped and the girls stepped off, Rachel's legs felt like two sticks of rubber. "Can we sit awhile?" she asked as they stepped up to Dave.

He shook his head. "I want to go on the Wild Mouse next."

"What's the Wild Mouse?" Rachel wanted to know.

Dave pointed straight ahead. "It's a wooden roller coaster with a lot of quick turns and drops that make your stomach do flip-flops."

Rachel's heart pounded. "M–maybe I should stay here and watch."

"Oh, no, Rachel, you have to go on the Wild Mouse with us," Sherry insisted. "It'll be so much fun; you'll see!"

"Oh, all right," Rachel finally agreed.

"Looks like there's quite a lineup," Dave said. "We may have to stand in line awhile."

Sherry groaned. "I hope the wait's not too long because I'm getting hungry."

Dave reached into his pocket and took out a pack of gum. "Here's something to tide you over until lunch." He handed a stick of gum to Sherry and one to Rachel.

"Thank you." Rachel popped the gum into her mouth and chewed.

Sherry wrinkled her nose. "Chewing gum won't take my hunger away."

Dave poked her. "Maybe not, but it'll keep your mouth busy so you can't complain."

She glared at him. "Very funny!"

"Make sure you spit the gum out before we get on the roller coaster," Dave said. "You might swallow it on one of those dips."

"Don't worry about me." Sherry returned the stick of gum. "Here you go, Dave. I'm not going to chew this!"

Dave shrugged and put the gum back in his pocket. "Suit yourself, picky little sister."

"I'm not picky!"

"Yeah, you are!"

Rachel bit back a smile. It seemed that she and Jacob weren't the only siblings who didn't always get along.

As they waited in line, Sherry continued to complain about being hungry. Rachel was too busy watching people and listening to the screams coming from the Wild Mouse to think about her empty stomach.

Finally, it was their turn to ride the roller coaster. Sherry and Rachel sat together, and Dave sat behind them with a young boy.

"Hang on tight and get ready to scream," Sherry hollered in Rachel's ear as the coaster moved forward. "This will probably be the most exciting part of your day!"

As the Wild Mouse climbed higher and higher, Rachel hung onto the bar in front of her until her knuckles turned white. Suddenly, the roller coaster made a sharp turn, and down. . .down they went!

Rachel's stomach seemed to fly up, and her breath caught in her throat. When she opened her mouth to scream—*gulp!*—her gum slid down her throat! She'd forgotten to spit it out.

She swallowed a couple more times. Then she clung tighter to the bar and screamed as the roller coaster dipped up and down and rocked side to side. No wonder they called it the Wild Mouse!

When the coaster stopped, Rachel's legs shook so much she could barely stand.

"That was sure fun! Let's get in line and go again!" Sherry shouted.

Dave looked at Sherry like he didn't believe her. "I thought you were hungry."

"I was, but my hunger's gone, and I want to ride again." Sherry looked at Rachel. "What about you? Wouldn't you like to ride the Wild Mouse one more time?"

Rachel shook her head. "I've had enough of wild rides for now. But if you two want to go again, I'll wait here for you."

"The line's gotten even longer, so it might be some time before we get on," Sherry said.

Dave handed Rachel a few dollars. "Why don't you get something to eat? If you'd like to look around a bit, that's okay, too." He glanced at his watch. "It's eleven thirty now, so make sure you're back here by twelve thirty. If our ride's over before then we may decide to go on something else, but we'll meet you here and then we'll have lunch."

"Okay, thank you." Rachel headed for the nearest stand selling cotton candy. She bought some and was about to sit on a bench when— *thunk!*—a teenage boy bumped her arm, and the cotton candy went right in her face!

"Sorry," he mumbled as he dashed away.

Rachel licked her lips to get the cotton candy off, but she could feel it on her cheeks and her nose. She ate the rest of the cotton candy and went to find a restroom.

After she'd washed the mess off her face, she looked for a drinking fountain. She bent over, took a drink, and let the cool water roll around on her tongue before she swallowed again.

An elderly couple walked by, and Rachel asked them, "Excuse me, but do you know what time it is?"

"Ten minutes to twelve," the man answered.

"Thanks." Rachel walked until she came to a sign pointing to Zoo America, which she realized was another part of the park. She remembered her cousin Mary saying in one of her letters that she'd visited a zoo in northern Indiana. It sounded like a lot of fun, and Rachel had been envious. Now she could visit a zoo, too.

Rachel followed the signs pointing to the zoo, but when she got to the entrance, she saw there was an admission fee. Since she'd spent the money Dave had given her on cotton candy, she couldn't go inside.

As Rachel walked away, she spotted a young boy eating a soft pretzel. *That pretzel sure looks good,* she thought. *I wish I had some money to buy one.*

She wandered on, her mouth watering as she watched people eating ice cream, popcorn, and caramel apples. Oh, how she wished she could buy something to eat.

She stopped to watch teenagers try to pop some balloons with darts. When she moved on she heard music and spotted a strolling guitar player and a man playing a drum.

Someone dressed in a candy bar costume asked if Rachel would like her picture taken. She shook her head and hurried on.

Next, she went into a gift shop where they sold T-shirts with the word "Hershey" written on the front. There were also a bunch of key chains and several shelves full of souvenirs.

I wonder what Jacob would say if he knew where I was, she wondered. *I'll bet he'd be jealous.*

Rachel could hardly wait to write Mary and tell her about the exciting time at Hershey Park! She was sure she would always remember this day.

Her stomach rumbled noisily. She stopped and asked another lady what time it was.

The woman looked at her watch. "It's twelve fifteen."

"Okay, thanks." Rachel decided to head back to the Wild Mouse roller coaster, figuring Sherry and Dave would be off the ride by now and were probably waiting for her. But when Rachel reached the Wild Mouse, she couldn't find Sherry or Dave. She wondered if they'd gone on another ride.

She nibbled on a fingernail. *Should I wait here or walk around some more?*

The sun beat on Rachel's head, and she wiped her sweaty forehead with the back of her hand. It had turned into such a sticky day! Maybe another drink of water would help.

Rachel spotted a drinking fountain and was almost there when she noticed some money on the ground.

She looked around, wondering who had dropped it, but the people walking by didn't seem to notice.

Rachel bent and snatched it up. Her mouth dropped open when she saw that it was a twenty-dollar bill! *With this much money I could buy something to eat,* she thought. *And since I don't know who dropped the money, I guess it's okay to keep it.*

She hurried to the nearest refreshment stand and bought a hot dog. She took a big bite. "Mmm... this tastes wunderbaar."

She still had plenty of money, so when she finished the hot dog she decided to play a few games of ring toss. She did quite well and had soon won a stuffed bear. Excited, she kept playing until she'd won a souvenir T-shirt and a matching hat.

Finally, the money was gone, so Rachel headed back to the Wild Mouse. She was disappointed to see that Dave and Sherry still weren't there.

She walked up to a teenage girl waiting in line

and said, "Do you know what time it is?"

The girl looked at her watch. "One o'clock."

Rachel's heart started to pound. It was thirty minutes past the time she was supposed to meet Sherry and Dave! Could they have left the park and gone home without her?

Chapter 11

Lost

Stay calm. Don't panic, Rachel told herself. *Sherry and Dave wouldn't have left without me. They must be here someplace. Oh, I hope they're still here.*

Rachel sat on a bench and placed the things she'd won beside her. She drew in a couple of shaky breaths. Dave had told her to meet them by the Wild Mouse roller coaster at twelve thirty. If he and Sherry had arrived at that time and had seen that she wasn't there, what might they have done?

Think, Rachel, think. Maybe they went looking for me. Maybe I should look for them. She rubbed her forehead and tried to relax. *But where? Hershey Park is so big. I might spend all day looking and never find them!*

An elderly woman sat beside Rachel. "It's sure warm today," she said, fanning her face with her hands.

Rachel nodded.

The woman frowned. "If I'd known it was going to be this hot I wouldn't have come here with my son and his family. I would have stayed home where it's air conditioned."

Rachel swallowed around the lump in her throat. "If I'd known I was going to lose my friends, I wouldn't have come here, either."

The woman raised her eyebrows. "Are you lost?"

Rachel shrugged. "I—I'm not really lost, but I was supposed to meet my friends here, and I don't know where they are."

The woman squeezed Rachel's arm. "Why don't we go to the Lost and Found booth? Maybe your friends are waiting there."

Hope welled in Rachel's chest. "Do you think so?"

"There's only one way to find out. Let's go see." The woman took Rachel's hand, and they walked through the crowd until they came to a booth marked Lost and Found.

"This young girl has lost her friends," the woman said to the man who sat behind the counter. "Has anyone been here looking for her?"

The man studied Rachel and shook his head. "No one I know of has asked about anyone who looks like you. What's your name?"

"Rachel Yoder."

"Sorry, but no one's come by asking for anyone by that name." The man motioned to a bench. "Why don't you have a seat and I'll call your friends' names over the loudspeaker? If they're in the park they should hear my message."

"O—okay." Rachel sat down and placed the things she'd won in her lap.

"What are your friends' names?" he asked.

"The girl's name is Sherry, and her brother is Dave."

"What's their last name?"

Rachel's forehead wrinkled as she tried to remember. She thought Sherry had mentioned her last name when they'd met at the farmer's market last summer, but she couldn't think of what it was. "I—uh—can't remember," she mumbled.

The man frowned and he looked at Rachel like he didn't quite believe her. "You don't know your friends' last name?"

She shook her head.

He shrugged and picked up the speakerphone. "Attention: Sherry and Dave. Would you please report to the Lost and Found to pick up your friend Rachel?" The man's voice boomed out over the speakers, and Rachel felt a surge of hope. If

Sherry and Dave were still in the park they were bound to hear their names being called and come to get her.

The elderly woman looked at her watch. "I'd like to wait with you, Rachel, but I'm supposed to meet my son and his family at Chocolate World in ten minutes."

"That's okay," Rachel said. "I'll be all right by myself."

"I'll keep an eye on Rachel until her friends arrive," the man behind the counter said.

The woman smiled and patted Rachel's shoulder. "You'll be found soon."

Rachel wished she felt as sure about things. She looked at the woman and forced a smile. "Thanks for helping me."

"You're welcome." The woman smiled and hurried away.

Rachel watched more people walk past. She hoped and prayed Sherry and Dave would come for her soon. She was getting ready to ask the man if he would call Sherry and Dave's names again when a young woman approached the building, pushing a baby stroller. Seeing the baby made Rachel think of Hannah, and a lump formed in her throat. Even though she didn't like being awakened at night when Hannah cried, and even though she felt ignored since the baby came home from the hospital, she missed her family and was worried that she might never see them again.

"My name's Sherry," the woman with the baby said to the man behind the counter. "Were you calling me over the loud speaker? I have a friend whose name is Rachel, but I don't think she's at Hershey Park today."

The man motioned to Rachel. "Do you know that little girl? She seems lost."

The woman looked over at Rachel, then back at the man, and shook her head. "Sorry, but I've never seen her." She looked at Rachel with sympathy. "I'm sure someone will come for you, though."

"I—I hope so."

The woman smiled at Rachel and walked away, pushing the baby stroller.

Rachel fidgeted on the bench as more people walked by, but still no Sherry and Dave. "Can you call my friends' names again?" she asked the man behind the counter.

He nodded and picked up the speakerphone. He'd just started to speak when a middle-aged man stepped up to the booth. "My name's Dave," he said. "Were you calling me?"

The attendant motioned to Rachel. "Do you know this young girl?"

The man shook his head. "Sorry, I don't."

"Then I guess you're not the Dave we're looking for."

Rachel's heart felt as if it had sunk all the way to her toes. Probably hundreds of people named Sherry and Dave were at Hershey Park. She could spend the rest of the day sitting here while the wrong Sherry and Dave came to see if their names had been called. The Sherry and Dave she knew might never show up.

Feeling more anxious by the minute, Rachel glanced around. She couldn't stay here. She had to find Sherry and Dave. She had to get home to her family!

When the man behind the counter was busy talking to someone else, Rachel scooped up the things she'd won, jumped off the bench, and ran as fast as she could. She ran all the way to the front gate of the park and waited for the tram to take her to the parking lot. She would go back to the spot where Dave had parked his car and wait for Dave and Sherry beside his car.

When Rachel stepped off the tram, she headed for

the spot where Dave had parked the car. Dave's car wasn't where he'd left it! At least she thought this was where he'd parked his convertible.

"They must have left without me!" she wailed. "They didn't hear their names because they're on their way home!"

Feeling as though the strength had drained from her legs, Rachel dropped the stuffed bear and other things to the ground and fell to her knees beside them. She clutched the bear to her chest. She sobbed until she could hardly breathe. She'd made a complete mess of things by getting into Dave's car and coming to Hershey Park. If only she hadn't been so foolish to think she needed a ride in a convertible. If she could turn back time she would have stayed home and spent the whole day cleaning. It would have been better than being alone in a strange place with a bunch of people she didn't know.

Once Rachel's sobs tapered to sniffling hiccups, she picked up her things and found a bench to sit on. Then she bowed her head and closed her eyes. *Dear Jesus, I'm all alone, and I need Your help. I miss my family—even my baby sister who cries too much.*

A song the scholars often sang at Rachel's school, about walking with Jesus whether we're walking in sunlight or shadows, popped into her head. *I might be lost,* Rachel continued to pray, *but I know You're here with me, Jesus. Please help me find some way to get home.*

She opened her eyes and saw an Amish family walking across the parking lot. A sense of hope welled in her soul. Maybe they lived in Lancaster County. Maybe they could help her get home!

Leaving the things she had won on the bench, Rachel dashed across the parking lot. Before she reached the Amish people, a group of teenagers got off the tram, blocking her view. By the time the crowd dispersed, the Amish family had gone.

Tears stung Rachel's eyes. *Will I ever see home again, or will I be stuck in this parking lot for the rest of my life?*

Chapter 12

Unexpected Surprise

A hopeless feeling swept over Rachel as she returned to the bench. She had prayed and asked God to help her. She knew Jesus hadn't left her. Yet she hadn't found Sherry and Dave, and she didn't know if she ever would. Should she go back to the Lost and Found booth, stay here, or what?

Tears welled in her eyes and she leaned forward, resting her head on her knees. *Please help me, Lord. Show me what to do.*

Tap...tap...tap. Someone tapped Rachel's shoulder. Her eyes snapped open, and she sat up. There stood Sherry and Dave!

Rachel jumped to her feet and threw her arms around Sherry. "I'm so glad to see you! I—I was afraid you'd gone back to Lancaster without me."

"Well, we should have!" Dave shook his finger at Rachel. "We heard our names being called over the loud speaker and went to the Lost and Found to get you, but when we got there you were gone."

"I—I waited a long time." Rachel's chin trembled and she sniffed. "When you didn't come, I decided to take the tram to the parking lot and wait for you by your car." She sucked in her breath. "Only your car wasn't there, and I was sure you'd gone home without me."

Dave scowled at her. "Leaving the park was a dumb idea! You should have stayed at the Lost and Found booth! What if we'd given up looking for you and had left you here?"

Tears streamed down Rachel's cheeks, and she wiped them with the back of her hand.

"You're lucky we decided to come out here looking for you!"

Sherry glared at her brother. "Stop shouting at Rachel! Can't you see how upset she is?" She gently patted Rachel's back, the way Mom often did. "Don't cry, Rachel. We're here now. Everything's okay."

"Are—are we going home?" Rachel asked.

Dave nodded. "I promised our folks we'd be back by supper, so we'd better leave now or we'll be late."

Rachel breathed a sigh of relief when she crawled into the backseat of Dave's convertible a few minutes later. God had answered her prayers. She was on her way home—going back to the family she loved. She had been foolish to want a ride in a convertible so much that she'd taken off without getting permission or letting anyone in the family know where she was going. Rachel knew she would be punished for her disobedience, but she also knew that what she'd done was wrong, so she deserved to be punished.

"Why didn't you wait for us in front of the Wild Mouse roller coaster?" Dave asked, looking over his shoulder at Rachel.

"I waited a long time there, too, but you never came." Rachel's throat felt raw and scratchy from crying so much, and she had a hard time swallowing. "Then a lady came along, and when I told her I couldn't find you, she took me to the Lost and Found."

"That's where you should have stayed," Dave said as he pulled out of the parking lot.

Sherry bumped his arm. "She panicked, Dave. Don't you realize how scared she was? Wouldn't you have been scared if you'd been in her situation?"

"Yeah, I guess so—at least when I was Rachel's age I would have been scared. I'm sorry for yelling," Dave called over his shoulder. "I was just worried because you'd run off."

"I–I'm sorry, too." Rachel blinked several times as more tears threatened to spill over. "I wish I'd never gone with you to Hershey Park."

"Didn't you have any fun today?" Sherry asked.

Rachel looked at the stuffed bear and other things she'd won, lying on the seat beside her. "I did have fun. . .until I couldn't find you and Dave."

"I'm sorry that happened," Sherry said. "We shouldn't have left you alone."

"That's all behind us now," Dave said. "Let's just relax and enjoy the ride home."

Rachel leaned against the seat and closed her eyes as the cool breeze blew against her face. In a while she would be home where she belonged.

Rachel had just drifted off when—*thump, thumpety, thump!*—the car shuddered and bumped along. Rachel knew something must be wrong.

Dave steered the car to the shoulder of the road. He got out, went to the passenger's side, and kicked the front tire. "That's just great! We'll be late getting home now for sure!"

Rachel sat up straight. "Wh–what's wrong?"

"I've got a flat tire!"

"Can it be fixed?"

"I can't fix the tire, but I do have a spare." Dave reached into his pants pocket and pulled out a cell phone.

"What are you doing?" Sherry asked.

"I'm calling Mom and Dad to let them know we're going to be late."

"That's a good idea," Sherry said.

Rachel thought about asking Dave if she could call her folks, but she changed her mind. It could be several hours, and maybe not until tomorrow, before someone in the family checked the answering machine in their phone shed.

When Dave hung up the phone, he went to the trunk of the car and got another tire. "You two will have to get out of the car while I change the tire."

"Can we help?" Sherry asked as she and Rachel scrambled out.

Dave shook his head. "Just stand back from the car and stay as far away from the road as you can. There's a lot of traffic, and I don't want either of you getting hit."

Sherry and Rachel did as Dave said. While they watched him change the flat tire, Rachel couldn't resist the urge to nibble a fingernail. It was getting late, and she knew Mom was probably home from town by now. She would have most likely read the note Rachel had left on the table and think she was still at Orlie's. When it was time to start supper and Rachel still wasn't home, Pap would probably go over to the Troyers' house to get her.

Rachel bit the end of two more fingernails. *Only I won't be there, and Orlie will tell Pap that I never went there.* Tears stung the backs of her eyes. *Will they be worried and think something bad happened? Will they search for me or call the sheriff?*

"Are you worried?" Sherry asked. "Sometimes I bite my nails when I'm worried about something."

Rachel studied her hands. Her fingernails didn't look very nice when she chewed them. "I know I shouldn't bite my nails," she said. "Mom tells me that whenever she catches me doing it, but I only bite my nails when I'm feeling nervous."

"Are you nervous right now?"

Rachel nodded.

Sherry draped her arm across Rachel's shoulders. "Don't be nervous. Dave will be finished with the tire soon and then we'll be on our way home."

"I'm gonna be in big trouble when my folks find out where I went." A tear slipped out of Rachel's eye and dribbled onto her cheek. "My brother calls me a little bensel, and I guess he's right."

"What's a bensel?" Sherry asked.

"A silly child." A few more tears fell, and Rachel wiped them with the back of her hand. "I'll never go anywhere again without my parents' permission."

"It's as much my fault as it is yours," Sherry said. "I shouldn't have invited you to go unless your folks were home and said it was all right."

Rachel shook her head. "It's not your fault."

"Yes, it is."

"No, I—"

"The tire's fixed!" Dave opened the car door. "So if you two will quit jabbering, we'll get back on the road."

Sherry wrinkled her nose. "You don't have to be so mean."

"Sorry," he mumbled, "but I'm feeling stressed right now."

Rachel could understand that. She felt stressed, too. But then she remembered what Grandpa had said about rejoicing in every circumstance—even in the midst of troubles, and she smiled. At least they would soon be home.

When Dave pulled his convertible into Rachel's driveway, her heart beat faster. He'd just turned off the engine when Mom and Grandpa rushed out of the house. Pap, Henry, and Jacob stepped out of the barn.

"Rachel, where have you been?" Pap shouted as Rachel, Sherry, and Dave got out of the car. "I just returned from Orlie's and he said you hadn't been to his house all day." He motioned to the phone shed. "I was about to phone the sheriff."

"Jah, and because of you taking off, we can't go to supper tonight," Jacob said, scowling at Rachel.

"You—you were going out to supper?" she asked.

Pap nodded. "We planned to take you out for a belated birthday supper, but now that will have to wait."

Rachel's eyes filled with tears. "I—I did something I shouldn't have done, and I'm so sorry."

"What did you do?" Mom asked, slipping her arm around Rachel's waist.

"I went to Hershey Park."

"Hershey Park?" Mom and Pap said at the same time.

Rachel nodded; then she motioned to Sherry and Dave. "This is Sherry and her brother Dave. I met Sherry at the farmer's market last summer, and I saw her again when Grandpa and I went to the

Bird-in-Hand restaurant a few weeks ago." Rachel gulped in a quick breath. "When I was heading to Orlie's to show him my new skateboard, Dave and Sherry drove by and stopped to say hello. Then they said—"

"We said we were going to Hershey Park, and I invited Rachel to join us," Sherry said.

Mom looked at Rachel and scowled. "And you agreed to go without getting our permission?"

Rachel nodded slowly. "I—I thought no one would miss me." She sniffed. "I thought no one cared about me anymore."

Henry shook his head. "That's just plain foolishness, Rachel. How could you even think such a thing?"

"Ever since Hannah came home from the hospital, everyone has made over her and ignored me—unless they wanted me to do some chore." *Sniff! Sniff!*

"It's true, we have made over the baby, and you have been asked to do more chores." Mom pulled Rachel to her side. "But it's not because we love Hannah more." She shook her head. "We love all our *kinner* [children] the same, and when there's work to be done, we're all expected to pitch in and help."

"That's right," Pap agreed. He moved closer to

Rachel. "If you felt no one cared about you, you could have said something so we could make things right instead of running off to Hershey Park."

Rachel nodded. "I know what I did was wrong, and I promise I'll never do anything like that again."

"I should hope not." Pap squeezed Rachel's shoulder. "We were very worried when we didn't know where you were. We were afraid something bad had happened to you."

"That's right," Jacob agreed. "Pap paced the barn floor after we got back from Orlie's."

"And your mamm was pacing inside the house," Grandpa said.

Mom nodded. "Jah, pacing and praying."

"While I was at Hershey Park I got separated from Sherry and Dave for a while," Rachel said. "I was praying then, too."

Grandpa patted Rachel's head. "And God brought you safely home to your family."

"Speaking of home," Dave spoke up, "Sherry and I need to go now. I don't want our folks to worry."

Rachel moved over to Sherry and hugged her. "Come by sometime and visit if you can."

Sherry nodded. "I'd like that. Maybe you can come to our place and visit me, too. We live in a big white house just down the road from the Plain and Fancy farm."

Rachel looked at Mom.

Mom shook her head. "I'm sorry, Rachel, but you won't be going anywhere except to church for the next several weeks. You'll not be allowed to have any company for a while, either."

Rachel didn't argue.

Sherry climbed into the car beside Dave. "Oh, Rachel, don't forget your skateboard and the stuffed animal and other things you won."

"I'll get my skateboard, but I don't want the other things," Rachel said. "Why don't you keep them?"

"Are you sure?"

Rachel nodded as Sherry handed her the skateboard. "I'm very sure."

"Thanks, Rachel." Sherry smiled as Dave started the car. "See you soon!"

Rachel turned and started for the house. "Is Hannah awake?" she asked Mom. "I'd like to hold her."

"She's sleeping right now, but you can hold her after supper," Mom said.

"And after you've washed and dried the dishes," Pap added.

Rachel nodded. She was so glad to be home she'd be willing to do any chore without complaint. Anything but feed and water Jacob's hairy mutt, that is.

"Before we go inside, I have something to give you," Grandpa said.

"What is it?" Rachel asked.

"It's a late birthday present. Remember when I told you a few weeks ago that I'd ordered something for your birthday but it hadn't arrived yet?"

She nodded. "I'd forgotten about it."

"Well, come with me, and I'll show you what I ordered." Grandpa led Rachel to his greenhouse. When he and Rachel stepped inside, he pointed to a box wrapped in white tissue paper. "Go ahead, Rachel. Open your gift."

Rachel tore the wrapping away from the box and opened it. When she lifted a wooden sign out of the box, her mouth dropped open. "Grandpa, this says *Grandpa and Rachel's Greenhouse.*"

Grandpa nodded. "That's right, Rachel."

"But I—I don't understand."

He patted her back. "Someday, when I retire,

this greenhouse will be yours."

Tears welled in Rachel's eyes, and she hugged Grandpa. "Danki, Grandpa. This is the best birthday present I've ever had; and being back home with my family makes it even more special."

As Rachel and Grandpa walked back to the house, she thought about the rest of summer. Even though she might not be able to go anywhere for several weeks, she would enjoy every day right here at home. And that was exactly where she belonged!

Also available from Barbour Publishing

School's Out!

RACHEL YODER—
Always Trouble Somewhere
Book 1
by Wanda E. Brunstetter
ISBN 978-1-59789-233-9

Back to School

RACHEL YODER—
Always Trouble Somewhere
Book 2
by Wanda E. Brunstetter
ISBN 978-1-59789-234-6

Out of Control

RACHEL YODER—
Always Trouble Somewhere
Book 3
by Wanda E. Brunstetter
ISBN 978-1-59789-897-3

New Beginnings

RACHEL YODER—
Always Trouble Somewhere
Book 4
by Wanda E. Brunstetter
ISBN 978-1-59789-898-0

A Happy Heart

RACHEL YODER—
Always Trouble Somewhere
Book 5
by Wanda E. Brunstetter
ISBN 978-1-60260-134-5